I0604122

The Manic Collective Candidate

Thomas Brant

Copyright © 2026 Thomas Brant.

All rights reserved.

No part of this book can be reproduced in any form or by written, electronic or mechanical, including photocopying, recording, or by any information retrieval system without written permission in writing by the author.

Published by T Brant Publishing

Printed in Great Britain

Unless otherwise indicated, all the names, characters, businesses, places, events and incidents in this book are either the product of the author's imagination or used in a fictitious manner. Any resemblance to actual persons, living or dead, or actual events is purely coincidental.

Although every precaution has been taken in the preparation of this book, the publisher and author assume no responsibility for errors or omissions. Neither is any liability assumed for damages resulting from the use of information contained herein.

Print ISBN 978-1-0683106-3-8

eBook ISBN 978-1-0683772-5-9

CHAPTER 1 - Decision Made
Monday 15th January 2024

The rush of preparation for the drivetime show on Manic Radio Essex, the regional brand that replaced the old Essex Beats, filled the studio with a familiar energy. Callie Hall knew that she had an hour until her drive time show was slated to start, as it, like several other shows on Manic's CHR brands, a mixture of heritage names from the former Breeze Media and Manic stations and rebranded stations that had been brought, like her own, from Lite Group two years earlier.

At 21, she was one of the younger batch of Manic presenters that had been poached from Bauer and Global's training programmes. While some of her colleagues had years of experience, she had come straight from Kiss Fresh, having done the early breakfast slot for a few months before Manic poached her. Now, she had a prime slot on Manic Radio Essex, covering the 4-7pm drive show. It was a gig that came with a significant audience, especially given how much Global's Heart Essex had lost traction since its networked format kicked in.

The irony that she was firmly within the demographic that Manic aimed for its contemporary hits radio brand, which was a 18-34 demographic, wasn't lost on her. She was exactly the kind of presenter that Manic wanted: young, energetic, social media savvy, and willing to push boundaries. And, unlike some of her colleagues who had been through the wringer of local radio's decline, she had no nostalgia for what had been lost. To her, Essex Beats was just an old name on an Ofcom licensing document. Manic was the future, and she was at the heart of it.

She knew that, living in Romford, that the local elections were a mere 5 months away, and that the Mayor, a useless (in her opinion) waste of space who, like the rest of the Labour Party, had done nothing to fix the things that really mattered. The state of the roads? A disaster. Public transport? A joke. And don't even get her started on the crime rates. But above all, the thing that really riled her up was the London-centric nature of everything.

Even though Romford was part of the London Borough of Havering, it never truly felt like London. It was too far east, too Essex, too overlooked. Whenever the Mayor spoke about "Londoners," he meant people in Zones 1 and 2—the ones who lived in overpriced flats and worked in media, politics, or finance. The ones who took the Tube everywhere and had never set foot in a Greggs past the M25.

She knew that the irony of her own position, Manic Radio Essex being based at the Olympic Park, meant that she was commuting into the very heart of what she despised. Yes, the commute on the Elizabeth Line meant that she could be at work in less than thirty minutes, and that it also meant that she could visit her brother in Shenfield by jumping on an Elizabeth Line train going the other way, but that wasn't the point. The point was that she resented the way everything in her world revolved around London. Essex had its own identity, its own culture, its own way of doing things. But it was always treated as an afterthought.

"You alright, Callie?" Daisy Round, one of the Medway Heatwave presenters, poked her head into the studio, holding a can of Monster and looking as if she'd barely slept. Callie knew that Daisy, at 24, was part of Manic's party culture, where sex, alcohol and cocaine were as common as the constant churn of TikTok trends. Daisy's dishevelled look wasn't surprising—she was known for doing her Medway Heatwave drive show half-hungover more often than not. Callie was the same, a cocaine addict and was as loose with her morals as a bag of chips left outside a Romford Wetherspoons on a Saturday night.

She grinned at Daisy, her fingers drumming against the desk as the idea that had been brewing in her head all weekend solidified into a plan. A ridiculous, chaotic, very Manic plan.

"Yeah, I'm good," she said, cracking open her own can of Monster. "Just thinking."

Daisy raised an eyebrow, taking a sip of her drink. "That's dangerous. What about?"

Callie smirked. "About how I'm gonna run for Mayor of London."

Daisy choked on her sip, coughing into her sleeve. "What?"

"Dead serious." Callie leaned forward, her eyes glinting with mischief. "Think about it. No one's actually voting for the Tories or Labour for any real reason. It's just vibes. And all the candidates are boring as fuck. I mean, Sadiq's been Mayor since before I even left school. No one cares anymore."

Daisy stared at her like she'd just suggested taking on Global by launching a Manic-sponsored OnlyFans. "Callie, babe. You present drive in Essex. That's not exactly a political background."

Callie shrugged. "Yeah, and? It's not like I'm trying to be Prime Minister. It's just the Mayor. And all I need is a stupid gimmick and people will eat it up." She cracked her neck. "If Count Binface can run against Khan in the last Mayoral election on a platform to rename London Bridge to "Phoebe Waller-Bridge" and Hammersmith Bridge to "Wayne Bridge", then surely I can run on a platform that actually means something to people like us."

Daisy shook her head, half-laughing. "And what's your genius campaign slogan, then? 'Manic's Better, Innit Babes'?"

Callie's grin widened. "Exactly that. I want to ban Capital."

Daisy nearly dropped her can. "Ban… Capital? As in, the radio station?"

"Yep." Callie leaned back in her chair, stretching her arms. "Think about it, Daisy. Capital's just boring now. Especially with that cunt on Breakfast."

Daisy blinked at her, trying to process what she'd just heard. "Wait, wait, wait. You're actually serious?"

"Deadly." Callie took another sip of her Monster and set the can down with a thud. "Capital's been shit for years. It's the same ten songs on repeat, the presenters have no personality, and don't even get me started on the fake caller competitions. Manic's taken over everywhere because people actually want a bit of chaos, a bit of fun. And let's be real—if Manic didn't exist, Capital would still be shoving Ed Sheeran down everyone's throats twenty times a day."

Daisy snorted. "They already do."

"Exactly! And it's not just that—it's the principle. Global basically owns commercial radio in London, and OFCOM lets them get away with it. Where's the competition? Where's the choice? They're even killing off Heart and making it all networked! Manic's the only thing actually keeping radio interesting." Callie sat forward, her hands animated. "Imagine it: a proper campaign, full of madness, a total piss-take but also something people can actually get behind. I'll be the candidate for the people who don't give a fuck about politics but know they're sick of the same old shit."

Daisy raised an eyebrow. "And you think people are gonna vote for you over, like, actual politicians?"

Callie scoffed. "People voted for Boris and look what that wanker did, partying during the pandemic while telling everyone else to stay at home. Ukraine elected a fucking comedian and he's fighting Russia while their actual politicians were too busy arguing about nonsense, and the Yanks elected Trump and Sleepy Joe. So yeah, I reckon I've got a shot."

Daisy exhaled through her nose, shaking her head. "Callie, this is next-level unhinged. I mean, I get it. It's very on-brand for you. But you do realise you'll need, like, actual policies? Not just 'ban Capital' and 'fuck Sadiq', right?"

Callie rolled her eyes. "Obviously. My other policies are free WKD to all uni students, banning council tax and defunding the police if they so much as do another Sarah Everard."

Daisy let out a low whistle, staring at Callie in something between disbelief and admiration. "Mate, you're actually going for it, aren't you?"

Callie leaned forward, the glint in her eye growing sharper. "I'm not just going for it, Dais. I'm making it happen. I'll get the signatures, I'll pay the deposit, and I'll be on that ballot. And trust me, people will listen. Manic's got the biggest audience in London outside of Global, and we know how to make noise. If we can get trending every time Kyler fucks up on air, we can definitely get me into the headlines."

Daisy sat back, folding her arms. "Alright, so let's say you actually pull this off. Let's say you run. Who's backing you? You need a party. Even Count Binface had the 'Count Binface Party'. What's yours?"

Callie grinned. "The Manic Collective."

Daisy nearly choked on her Monster again. "You're actually naming it after the station?"

Callie shrugged. "Why not? Manic's all about chaos and disruption, right? It's what we do best. Anyway, Legal at HQ in Speke have given it the nod, so I can use the station's name in the party, and they've allocated a provisional £200k for campaigning costs. Plus, Adam Banks thinks it'll be great PR. He reckons we'll get at least a million quids' worth of media coverage just from the backlash alone."

Daisy let out a low whistle, shaking her head in disbelief. "Callie, this is either the dumbest thing you've ever done or the most genius. I genuinely can't tell."

Callie smirked, downing the last of her Monster and tossing the empty can into the bin. "It's both. But mostly genius."

Daisy still looked sceptical. "Alright, so you've got HQ's backing, you've got a name, and you've got a gimmick. But do you actually know how to register as a candidate? Like, legally?"

Callie waved a hand dismissively. "Obviously. I Googled it."

Daisy snorted. "And what did the great oracle of the internet tell you?"

"I need to be over 18—sorted. A British citizen—obviously. And I need to get 330 nominations—ten from each borough of London—sorted, as most of the staff here live in the various London boroughs. And finally, a £10,000 deposit, which Manic's covering." Callie smirked. "Easy."

Daisy shook her head, still half in disbelief. "And that's it? That's all it takes to run for Mayor of London? No actual experience needed?"

Callie scoffed. "Babe, do you think half the people running have experience? They just slap a logo on a leaflet and say some buzzwords. At least I've got an actual following. And let's be real, this whole thing's a joke anyway. The whole system's a joke. I'm just playing the game better."

Daisy leaned back in her chair, a slow grin spreading across her face. "Alright, I'll admit it. This is next-level chaos. But also, I kinda love it."

Callie shot her a knowing look. "Exactly. You're gonna help me, right?"

Daisy groaned. "Fuck's sake, Callie."

Callie wiggled her eyebrows. "Come on. Think about it. We get to wind up Global, take the piss out of the election, and maybe—just maybe—actually make a point while we're at it. What's not to love?"

Daisy exhaled sharply, shaking her head with a chuckle. "Fine. But only because I wanna see how much we can get away with before OFCOM throws a fit."

Callie grinned triumphantly. "That's the spirit."

At that moment, her producer, Jordan McCabe, stuck his head into the studio. "Hey Daisy, Murph say's he needs a shag, and he's missing your half-empty bottle of Jäger from last night. He says if you don't return it, he's sending your hungover arse on street team duty for the next week. Anyway, what are you two witches brewing?"

Callie turned in her chair, her grin widening at Jordan's interruption. "Just a little campaign planning, babes."

Jordan rolled his eyes, clearly unimpressed. "Oh yeah? And what are you running for? Queen of the Essex slags?"

Daisy cackled, nearly spilling what was left of her Monster. "Nah, she's going for Mayor of London."

Jordan stared blankly for a moment, then burst out laughing. "Piss off."

Callie folded her arms, her smirk unwavering. "Dead serious."

Jordan's laughter faded as he realised, she wasn't joking. "You're actually doing this?"

Callie nodded. "Mate, Global needs taking down a peg, and I'm the one to do it. Plus, people love a bit of chaos. Look at who's actually running—Sadiq again, some Tory no one cares about, no doubt the little Hitlers at Britain First and Farage's gangbangers."

"Ah, Reform, the party for the gammon who think Wetherspoons is fine dining, and the Daily Mail is gospel," Jordan finished with a smirk. "You might actually have a point, Callie."

Callie leaned back, tapping her nails against the desk. "Exactly. I mean, let's be real, I'm not actually gonna win. But if we make enough noise, Manic will be all over the news. We'll be in the Standard, the Mail, maybe even on Piers Morgan's show. And Global? They'll absolutely shit themselves. I mean, Capital is Ashley Tabor-King's baby, and hearing it be banned by a candidate on the Mayoral ballot? That'll have them scrambling. Even if it's a joke campaign, it's a joke they won't be laughing at."

Jordan snorted, shaking his head in disbelief. "Mate, this is actually insane. But you know what? I reckon you could actually pull it off. At least the media circus bit."

Callie shrugged. "That's all I need. Get my name out there, rile people up, and make some noise. Worst-case scenario? I get booted out in the first round and still end up with 100k new followers and a load of press. Best-case scenario? We send Global into meltdown."

"It's not being done by rounds," Laurence Kendal, one of the technicians who was ensuring that the RCS Zetta systems that the Olympic Park studios used were actually working, cut in from the doorway, looking vaguely intrigued despite himself. "It's first past the post now. No more ranked-choice voting. So, if you get enough pissed-off Manic listeners to back you, you might actually have a shot at beating some of the joke candidates."

"Imagine if Binface or whatever gammon Farage or Britain First put forward ends up with fewer votes than me," Callie cackled. "That would be the biggest embarrassment in British politics since Liz Truss's lettuce."

"To be fair, babes," Daisy said with a grin, "Truss was the biggest embarrassment since Boris Johnson got stuck on that zip line waving Union Jacks like a Poundland Prince William."

The whole studio burst into laughter, even Laurence, who rarely found anything amusing unless it involved someone at Global getting humiliated.

Jordan let out a low whistle. "That's a big ask. You'd need, what, at least a few thousand votes to avoid being completely rinsed?"

Callie shrugged. "Easy. Manic's got a massive audience across London and Essex. We push the campaign on social, hammer it on air, get people talking. Doesn't even matter if they think it's a joke. Enough people putting my name down just for the banter, and boom—I'm above Britain First and Reform."

Daisy took another sip of her Monster, shaking her head with amusement. "You realise if you actually get enough traction, the press are gonna dig into everything you've ever done, right? They'll find every dodgy tweet, every messy night out, every time you slagged off another station on air."

Callie waved a dismissive hand. "Babe, have you met me? That's literally my brand. The public will eat it up. 'Local Essex Girl Takes on the Establishment'—proper tabloid gold."

Jordan checked his phone and let out a chuckle. "Speaking of, it's already starting. Someone's posted a screenshot of your Instagram story from last night where you wrote, 'Capital FM is an abomination that should be set on fire'. It's getting traction on Twitter."

Callie grinned at the news, grabbing her phone and flicking through Twitter. Sure enough, her Instagram story had made its way onto a trending thread, with responses ranging from absolute horror to outright hilarity.

"This is why Manic presenters need to be muzzled."

"Capital FM should issue a restraining order at this point."

"Not gonna lie, if she actually runs on this platform I might vote for her."

She turned her phone around so Daisy and Jordan could see. "See? It's working already. I haven't even announced my candidacy yet, and people are talking."

Jordan whistled, shaking his head. "Either you're a genius or you've finally lost it. But either way, I'm here for it."

Daisy leaned back, looking at Callie with an expression halfway between admiration and exasperation. "So, what now? What's the next step in this master plan of yours?"

Callie cracked her knuckles. "Well, I need to actually make it official. That means getting those signatures sorted, setting up a campaign website, and finding someone to manage the social media push. I also need to film a proper announcement video—something catchy, something that'll grab attention." She tilted her head, considering. "Maybe we film it outside Global's HQ. Get a big banner that says, 'Time's up, Capital.'"

Jordan snorted. "Yeah, because that definitely won't get you a cease-and-desist before you even get started."

Callie shrugged. "Cease-and-desist means they're scared. And that's half the fun."

Daisy exhaled through her nose. "Fine. But if we're doing this, we're doing it properly. You need a proper campaign video. Not just you standing outside Global HQ talking shit."

Callie nodded. "Obviously. I was thinking more of a dramatic montage. Shots of me walking through the streets of London like I'm a revolutionary. Maybe some clips of people shaking their heads at overpriced train tickets and potholes. Then I come in with the voiceover: 'London is broken. And you know what? So is its radio.'"

Jordan chuckled. "You know, my brother's a film studies student at Ravensbourne. He's got a proper camera and editing kit. He's also got a drone for those dramatic aerial shots. If you want something that looks semi-professional instead of your usual iPhone rant, I can get him to film it."

Callie's eyes lit up. "Now we're talking. Get your brother on the phone, tell him we need the full works. Drone shots, moody slow-motion, proper cinematic stuff. If I'm gonna make a scene, I want it to be a masterpiece."

Daisy groaned, rubbing her temples. "This is going to be the biggest shitshow in London politics since, well… the last election."

Callie grinned. "That's the plan."

Jordan tapped at his phone, already sending a message to his brother. "Alright, I'll see if he's up for it. But you're paying him."

Manic's covering campaign costs," Callie shot back smugly. "If they can throw money at a promo for Kyler's new podcast that nobody's listening to, they can throw some at making me look like the second coming of Guy Fawkes. They're also giving me a 12 episode podcast deal for after the election."

Daisy let out a low whistle. "Twelve episodes? They're really betting on you making a splash."

Callie smirked. "Of course they are. Even if I don't win, this is going to be the biggest media circus London's seen in years. Manic's all about getting noticed, and if I'm out there making headlines, that's good for them."

Jordan shook his head in disbelief. "You really think you can get enough people to take this seriously?"

Callie leaned forward, her eyes gleaming. "It doesn't have to be serious. It just has to be loud. Think about it—every other candidate is playing the same old game. I'm giving people something different. Something fun. People are sick of politics as usual, sick of the same faces, the same bullshit promises. They want someone who actually gets them. And if that person happens to be a 21-year-old Manic presenter who openly admits to being a chaotic mess? Even better."

Daisy raised an eyebrow. "You're basically running on a platform of 'I'm just like you lot, but with a microphone.'"

"Exactly." Callie grinned. "It's like how Trump got elected by acting like a reality TV villain, or how Boris won because he played up the bumbling idiot act. People love a character. And let's be honest, British politics is already a joke. I'm just making it an entertaining one."

Jordan's phone buzzed, and he glanced down. "My brother's in. He says he'll bring his camera kit down to Olympic Park tomorrow night."

Callie clapped her hands together. "Perfect. That gives me 24 hours to sort the script. I want this to be cinematic as fuck."

Daisy chuckled. "You mean you want to be the Essex Guy Fawkes."

Callie winked. "Exactly. Time to blow up the establishment—metaphorically, obviously."

Jordan exhaled sharply. "Mate, you might want to be careful with your wording before the Met put you on a watchlist."

Callie waved him off. "Oh please, the Met are too busy covering up their own scandals to care about me. Besides, they're more likely to arrest me for being 'too loud and having too much fun' than anything serious."

Daisy leaned back, shaking her head. "I can't believe I'm saying this, but… I think you might actually pull this off."

Callie smirked. "Of course I will. Now, who's in charge of getting me a fake podium for this video? I want it to look like I'm making a proper announcement."

Jordan groaned. "Why do I feel like I'm about to regret this?"

"Because you probably are," Daisy muttered. "But it's going to be fucking hilarious."

Callie cracked open another can of Monster, leaning back with a satisfied grin. "Right then. Let's make history."

****

CHAPTER 2 – The Manic Battle Bus
Wednesday 17th January 2024

Callie had to laugh at the battle bus that had just pulled into the Olympic Park car park. It was completely ridiculous.

A massive, bright neon orange Dennis Trident, one that was older than her, being a TfL castoff from the early 2000s, had been repainted in Manic's neon orange colours, one of the three main colours that the station used for its contemporary hits radio brands, along with neon pink and neon green, depending on the station and area that it covered, completely devoid of any text or imagery, just the base colour of orange and, surprisingly, a large box of spray paint in various colours in the luggage bay at the front of the bus.

Callie squinted at the bus, shielding her eyes from the glare of the garish orange paint in the weak winter sunlight. It looked like something out of a fever dream. The sheer absurdity of it was exactly what she'd hoped for.

Jordan whistled low as he walked around it, hands shoved into his hoodie pockets. "Mate, this is giving Year 9 art project vibes."

Daisy folded her arms, nodding in agreement. "I love how it's all sleek and corporate in neon orange, but then… what's with the spray paint?" She nudged Callie. "You planning on tagging your own battle bus?"

"Yeah. Kez from PR said to do our own design, and they'll add the corporate and legal bits after," Callie said, shaking the can of spray paint she'd just pulled from the box. "Apparently, they think it'll make it look more 'authentic.' Like some kind of street-level grassroots movement rather than a multi-million-pound radio stunt. To be fair, I'd rather have it look like it's been parked in Romford or Barking for a month than have a polished corporate campaign bus like I'm some stuck-up career politician. We're Manic. We do things messy."

Jordan snorted. "Yeah, messy is definitely the word for this." He rapped his knuckles against the side of the bus. "Bet this thing still smells like school trips to the Science Museum."

Daisy leaned in, wrinkling her nose. "Nah, mate. Smells like broken heaters and lost Oyster cards."

Callie opened the doors using the emergency button and boarded it, only for the smell of clean, fresh leather on the seats, and the unmistakable chemical tang of industrial-strength air freshener to hit her. She coughed, waving a hand in front of her face.

"Jesus, they've actually tried to clean it. What's the point of having an old London bus if it doesn't smell like fags, McDonald's, and despair?"

Jordan followed her in, raising an eyebrow as he took in the new upholstery. "They've done it up nice, though. Doesn't feel like a corpse of a 2003 school trip anymore."

Daisy flopped onto one of the seats, stretching out. "Bit weirdly posh, considering the outside looks like it was dunked in Fanta." She tapped the seat next to her. "I like it. Feels ironic."

"You know we've got a PR guy who owns a bus on the payroll," Callie said with a chuckle. "You know, the one who we take the piss out of because he shares a name with him off Top Gear. He said he'll be driving it for me... and apparently it's a convertible open topper too."

"Ah, Hammond, the lanky bastard who loves transport more than his own family," Jordan finished, shaking his head with a grin. "Manic really went all out, huh?"

Callie nodded, tossing the spray can between her hands. "Yeah, mate. Apparently Manic own this bus and have it as their promo bus for Christmas up in Glasgow, according to Hammond. They had it decked out in fairy lights and fake snow for some Christmas roadshow thing last month, going round all the Scottish towns and doing outside broadcasts with Santa and freebie giveaways. They must've driven it straight down from Glasgow just for this."

"No wonder... I've just found some tinsel," Daisy said with a laugh, pulling a stray bit of silver tinsel from the seat beside her. She twirled it between her fingers before tossing it at Callie. "Might as well keep it, babes. Bit of festive cheer for your campaign."

Callie caught the tinsel mid-air, shaking her head. "Yeah, nothing says 'serious political movement' like leftover Christmas decorations. Might as well shove Santa in as my deputy while we're at it."

Jordan plopped himself down in the driver's seat, pressing random buttons on the old control panel. "So, this is officially the 'Manic Battle Bus'? Like, what's the plan? Are we just driving around London, blasting music and slagging off Global?"

Callie smirked. "Pretty much. Except instead of just music, we're setting up mini pop-up raves, getting listeners involved, and causing absolute chaos everywhere we go. We'll stop off in key boroughs, do some outside broadcasts, and take the piss out of every other mayoral campaign in the process."

Jordan raised an eyebrow. "So, basically, this is less 'political campaign' and more 'Manic's loudest-ever PR stunt'?"

Daisy leaned back in her seat, grinning. "And you expected anything else?"

Callie reached for a can of orange spray paint, shaking it aggressively. "Right, let's get this thing looking proper. I don't want some clean-cut campaign bus. I want it looking like it's been hijacked by a bunch of ASBO kids from Romford."

"Hey, how about we head upstairs first, see what kit is up there?" Jordan suggested, already bounding up the stairs with the energy of a kid on a school trip.

Callie and Daisy followed, and as they reached the top deck, they were met with a complete difference to the downstairs section, with only two pairs of seats at the front, and the rest made up of a bar style area and a DJ booth.

Callie let out a low whistle, taking in the unexpected transformation of the upper deck. "Well, well, well. Now *this* is more like it."

Daisy leaned against the rail, peering around with a raised eyebrow. "They've actually turned it into a rave bus? I thought you were taking the piss when you said pop-up parties."

Jordan spun around in the DJ booth chair, flicking a couple of switches that made LED strips along the edges of the ceiling glow a deep, pulsing orange. "Mate, they really went all in. We've got decks, a proper mixer… even a fog machine. We could do a full-on illegal rave with this thing."

Callie grinned, running her hand over the surface of the bar-style seating. "It's like they want me to get arrested."

Daisy plopped onto one of the front seats, stretching her legs across the aisle. "I mean, I don't hate it. But I feel like someone at HQ is giving you just enough rope to hang yourself."

Callie rolled her eyes, pulling out her phone and snapping a few pictures. "Babe, they're investing in my success. Or, at the very least, in the chaos that comes with it. Either way, it's a win for Manic."

Jordan leaned back in the DJ chair, drumming his fingers against the desk. "So, what's the actual plan then? Are we just driving around London like a mobile festival, or are we going full 'political movement' with it?"

Callie smirked. "Both. We'll hit up all the boroughs, get listeners involved, do impromptu live sets, and generally make a spectacle. Think pirate radio energy but with a legal loophole." She waved a hand at the bus. "We'll throw some campaign speeches in for good measure, but let's be real—no one's tuning in for that."

"Don't you need to announce your candidacy and get the nominations paperwork done?" Jordan asked, spinning lazily in the DJ chair. "Pretty sure you can't just turn up at City Hall with a boombox and a vibe check."

"I'm doing the announcement on air on Friday, and I've got until March to get the paperwork handed in at City Hall," Callie replied, checking her phone to confirm the dates. "Which gives us plenty of time to cause a bit of mayhem before we go all official."

Callie cracked her knuckles, still grinning as she surveyed the top deck of the Manic Battle Bus. This wasn't just some half-baked campaign gimmick—this was a movement. Or at least, it would be once they got some proper graffiti on the outside and figured out where the hell they were going to park this thing without getting a fine.

Jordan leaned back in the DJ chair, stretching his arms behind his head. "Alright, so let me get this straight. The plan is: drive around London in this monstrosity, blast music, chat shit about Global, and somehow convince enough people to put a tick next to your name on election day?"

Callie grabbed a can of neon pink spray paint, shaking it aggressively. "Essentially, yeah."

Daisy snorted. "Mate, you need an actual slogan. Something that fits the 'Manic brand' but also doesn't make you sound like a complete joke."

Callie thought for a second before she grinned. "How about—'Manic's Better, Innit!"

Jordan and Daisy laughed at her, shaking their heads in disbelief.

Jordan wiped a tear from his eye. "Mate, that's the most Romford thing I've ever heard in my life."

Daisy tilted her head, considering. "It's catchy. It's dumb. It's absolutely you." She stretched out her arms. "Alright, let's get this bus looking like a riot on wheels before we take it for a spin."

Callie gave the can of neon pink spray paint an aggressive shake, then leaned in to tag the side of the bus. With a dramatic flourish, she sprayed "Manic's Better, Innit!" across the metal in huge, chaotic letters, letting the paint drip just enough to make it look raw and unpolished.

Jordan stepped back, nodding in approval. "That is peak Romford energy, mate."

Daisy twirled a can of neon green in her hand. "Alright, but we need more than just that. How about we throw in some slogans? Like, proper political ones."

Callie smirked. "Like what? 'Vote Callie, Get Pissed'?"

Jordan cackled. "Oi, honestly, you'd probably win South London on that alone."

"What about 'Sadiq's Had His Turn, Now It's Ours'?" Daisy suggested, shaking her can of neon green.

Callie considered it, tapping her fingers against the side of the bus. "Bit long. Needs to be snappier."

Jordan grinned, pointing at the top of the bus. "How about 'Make London Manic'?"

Daisy nodded. "Short, catchy, and vaguely threatening. Love it."

"You know, we need a Capital sticker on the side so we can spray a big red X over it," Callie said, snapping her fingers as the idea struck. "Properly hammer the message home. Nothing subtle—just full-on, blatant radio warfare."

"That's not a bad idea," a new voice, which made Callie chuckle, said. She knew who had arrived to join the party, as his show had finished an hour earlier and he had no doubt finished his post-show debriefing.

Kyler Thompson.

Callie knew Kyler was the biggest red flag in existence, despite being in his mid-20s and clearly still carrying himself like a chaotic teenage TikToker. The bleach-blond hair of the Manic Radio South Coast breakfast show was slightly dishevelled from his headphones, and his usual cocky grin was plastered across his face as he leaned against the side of the bus, arms crossed.

"Hey Daisy," Kyler said with a lecherous grin that Callie knew was about as subtle as a sledgehammer to the face. "Looking fresh as ever. Late night, was it?"

Daisy rolled her eyes. "Kyler, mate, if you try it on with me one more time, I'm gonna spray-paint 'Sex Pest' on your forehead."

Kyler cackled, unfazed. "Fair play, fair play. But come on, you lot are actually pulling this off? A full-blown campaign bus? I thought this was just Callie being Callie."

Callie tossed him a can of spray paint. "Oh, it's very much me being me. But now it's me, Manic, and an entire city's worth of pissed-off radio listeners. So, you in?"

Kyler twirled the can in his hand, pretending to think about it. "You know what? I like chaos. And pissing off Global? Even better."

Callie smirked as Kyler twirled the can of neon blue spray paint between his fingers like he was in some kind of Guy Ritchie film. He was an insufferable twat, but if there was one thing he was good at, it was causing trouble, and that was exactly what she needed right now.

"You better be in, mate," she said, cracking open another can of neon green. "Because this is gonna be the biggest piss-take London's seen since Boris got stuck on that zipline."

Kyler grinned, stepping forward and shaking the spray can. "Alright, alright. I'll bite. But only if I get to do something properly scandalous. Like… I dunno… climb on top of this thing in Trafalgar Square with a megaphone and scream 'Oi Sadiq, your time's up, babes!'"

Daisy groaned. "Christ, we're actually gonna end up on the front page of the Evening Standard, aren't we?"

Jordan snorted. "If we don't, we're doing it wrong."

Callie took a step back, admiring the freshly defaced battle bus. It was a riot of colour now, the sleek neon orange shell now slathered in chaotic graffiti. Some of it was strategic—big, bold slogans like Make London Manic and No More Boring Radio—but most of it was just pure nonsense. Daisy had scrawled Council Tax is a Scam across the back doors. Jordan had added Reform Are Just Gammon With WiFi near the front. And Kyler, of course, had drawn a very crude and anatomically incorrect phallic symbol on the emergency exit.

Callie smacked him round the head. "Oi, mate, I'm trying to run for office, not get us slapped with an obscenity fine."

Kyler cackled, ducking out of reach. "What? Politics is dick-measuring anyway."

Daisy rolled her eyes. "And somehow, he's still employed."

"Speaking of," Jordan said, checking his phone. "Hammond just messaged. He's nearly here to take this monstrosity for a test drive."

Callie clapped her hands together. "Perfect. Let's see what this bad boy can do."

They all piled onto the bus just as Hammond—Richard Hammond, Manic's resident transport nerd, not that Richard Hammond—came striding across the car park. Tall, lanky, and always slightly exasperated, he took one look at the freshly vandalised battle bus and sighed.

"What the fuck have you done to my bus?"

Callie grinned. "Improved it."

Hammond pinched the bridge of his nose like he was debating whether this job was worth it. "You do realise I actually have to drive this thing through London, yeah? Past actual police officers?"

Jordan patted his shoulder sympathetically. "Yeah, good luck with that, mate."

Hammond muttered something under his breath about regretting his life choices, then climbed into the driver's seat. He gave the engine a few revs, and the whole bus rumbled to life, vibrating beneath them.

Callie grinned. "Right, let's take this thing for a spin."

Hammond pulled out of the car park, the battle bus lurching forward with all the grace of a drunken giraffe.

The moment they hit the Stratford high street, people started staring. It was impossible not to. A massive neon-orange bus, covered in graffiti, blaring Manic Radio from the rooftop speakers like some sort of dystopian ice cream van—it was a spectacle, and Callie loved it.

****

"Y'know, Kyler," Callie said later that evening, when she had finished her show and met up with Kyler, who she knew had his 5 year old son, Link, spending time with his mother, Manic network host Toni Green, who lived in Liverpool and was divorced from Kyler. They were sitting in the upstairs section of a half-empty Wetherspoons in Stratford, nursing pints of overpriced lager while Callie scrolled through Twitter, grinning at the chaos they'd already managed to stir up. The battle bus had barely made it half a day on the streets of London before it started trending, with pictures flooding social media of the garish neon-orange monstrosity trundling past Westfield, graffiti splashed across its side like some kind of anarchist's fever dream. "There's a reason I want to ban Capital, apart from it being a right pile of shite, obviously."

Kyler raised an eyebrow, taking a sip of his pint. "Oh yeah? I assumed it was just because you've got some personal beef with Global."

Callie shrugged, spinning her phone between her fingers. "Well, yeah, obviously, but it's deeper than that. You know Roman Kemp, right?"

Kyler snorted. "Oh, here we go. What's Roman done now? Steal your Monster stash? Block you on Twitter? Forget to pay you back for a round?"

Callie rolled her eyes. "Nah, it's worse than that. I made a pass at him once. Like, proper shot my shot."

Kyler nearly choked on his drink. "No. Way."

Daisy, who had just returned from the bar with another pint for herself and a double vodka Red Bull for Callie, slid into the seat opposite them with a knowing smirk. "Oh, I've heard this story before. It's even funnier the second time."

Kyler leaned forward, grinning. "Alright, I need details. When was this? Where? How tragic was it on a scale of one to 'I never wanna talk about this again'?"

Callie groaned, rubbing her temples. "It was last year, alright? We were at some industry event, one of those pointless Global and Bauer networking dos where everyone pretends to be mates while secretly wishing each other's stations would go bust. Anyway, I'd had a few, felt a bit brave, thought, 'Sod it, why not?' He's good-looking, he's famous, and he's, y'know, not a total knob."

Kyler was already laughing. "And?"

Callie scowled. "And he rejected me. Politely. Which somehow made it worse."

Daisy cackled. "Yeah, he hit her with the classic 'Ahh, you're great, but I just don't see you that way' line."

Kyler whistled, shaking his head. "Oof. Brutal. You got 'friendzoned by a Kemp' energy now."

Callie groaned, slumping back in her seat. "Yeah, yeah, laugh it up. But that's not even the worst part. He did the whole 'I respect you too much' thing, as if he's some kind of untouchable saint. And then, not even a month later, he's all over some influencer type who looks like she exclusively eats kale and gets paid to breathe on Instagram."

Kyler winced. "Yeah, that's a rough one."

Callie jabbed a finger into the table. "So yeah, maybe I'm just a bit salty. But also, let's be real—Capital's been on life support for years. They just recycle the same ten songs and let Global run it like some kind of corporate cult. It's all sterile and boring and fake. Manic's the only station actually keeping radio interesting."

Kyler nodded. "Alright, I get it. But banning them? Seems a bit extreme."

Callie smirked. "It's not really about banning them, is it? It's about making noise. Getting people talking. Capital's the safe, corporate, polished option. Manic's the messy, unpredictable, slightly unhinged alternative. This is about drawing that line in the sand."

Daisy raised an eyebrow. "And also about getting back at Roman Kemp."

Callie shrugged. "Hey, if I happen to make his life slightly inconvenient in the process, that's just a happy bonus."

Kyler leaned back, swirling his pint. "So, what's the next step then? We've got the battle bus, we've got the campaign slogan, and you've got your weird personal vendetta. What now?"

Callie checked her phone, grinning at the messages from Manic HQ. "Now? We take this circus on the road."

****

CHAPTER 3 – Announcing on Air
Friday 19th January 2024

By the time Friday rolled around, the Manic Battle Bus was already infamous. It had been spotted all over London, from Stratford to Camden, from Croydon to Ealing, blasting Manic Radio at full volume and causing minor traffic chaos wherever it went. Social media was ablaze with pictures and videos of the neon-orange monstrosity, tagged with captions like *"What fresh hell is this?"* and *"Only in London."*

The hype was real. Callie Hall was not just the quirky drive-time presenter with a thing for chaotic PR stunts anymore—she was now a full-blown political force to be reckoned with, whether she liked it or not. The Battle Bus had given her a kind of instant visibility that many seasoned politicians would give anything for.

Callie, for her part, was loving every second of it. It was exactly what she'd wanted: the loudest, most absurd entry into the London Mayoral race.

Today, however, she was doing something different to her normal drive show. Instead of being exclusively on the Manic Radio Essex feed, she was on the quartet of London stations Manic owned: East London Hits, which covered Barking, Walthamstow, Stratford, and Ilford; South London Vibes, reaching Croydon, Brixton and Wimbledon (and until 2022, based out of a tiny studio above a Turkish barbers in Croydon High Street); North London Vibes, broadcasting to Barnet, Finchley, and Enfield, formerly a station based near Finchley Road Overground Station, and the main London Vibes station, which covered the entire M25 region, and, until 2022, had been based at 4 Golden Square.

Callie knew from her time at Kiss, which was based at No. 1 Golden Square, that London Vibes, during the Coronavirus Pandemic, had been a joke of an outfit, a glorified playlist service run on skeleton staff and PlayoutONE, a software service which had all the personality of a microwave on shuffle.

Then in June 2022, as part of preparations for the Lite Group-Manic merger, London Vibes had moved to Stratford, where East London Hits had been the main resident, part of a former Breeze Media secondary network centre within the Olympic Park complex. The technicians, at the time, were moving out, as Speke, the official network centre, was being made the primary and only operational base for everything above regional level, with stations that were based in the Meridian and LWT, as that was what OFCOM called the region, based on the ITV names, all moving their studios to the Stratford 30 studio hub, a complex which was made so by the removal of server racks, the underground Barbican style bowl for Manic Classical, and the installation of sleek new production suites, all retrofitted with the latest RCS Zetta playout systems, Sonifex desks, and noise-cancelling soundproofing.

As the site was still technically leased by the former Breeze Media and not Manic, the RCS system had been allocated, meaning that presenters from the former Lite stations, who had used Myriad, and former Manic sites, who used PlayoutONE, were now all working from the same platform, which led to a bit of an awkward transition for the presenters. The twin hub, Dudley, was the same, while other hubs had either Myriad or PlayoutONE in place, creating a real mishmash of systems that would take time to fully integrate. Coming from Bauer, however, and specifically Kiss Fresh, a graduate of the Bauer Academy before she had moved into the main Bauer then Manic fold, Callie was no stranger to these kinds of transitions. But today wasn't about technicalities—it was about causing a bloody scene.

"Alright, let's do this," Callie muttered to herself as she prepared for her announcement. The studio at Stratford had been transformed into a temporary makeshift war room. Neon lights flickered in the corner, reflecting the chaos that had become Callie's new normal. The Battle Bus, still parked outside with its spray-painted slogans flashing in the distance, was the symbol of the next phase in her campaign.

Looking at her co-host for the show, a veteran of East London Hits, Shanice Turner, the drive host on the station which had, until after the 2012 Olympics as Docklands Beats, Callie knew that the more experienced woman was rolling her eyes at the unfolding spectacle. Shanice had been around long enough to see plenty of ridiculous stunts in her career, but this? This was on another level.

"Another idiot who thinks she can blag her way into the mayoral race, huh?" Shanice muttered under her breath, her arms crossed as she watched Callie adjust the microphone. "This is either going to be a masterstroke or a complete car crash."

Callie shot her a grin, unbothered by the subtle shade. "You know what they say, Shan. Go big or go home." She motioned toward the window, where the Battle Bus gleamed in all its fluorescent glory, a true testament to her brand of chaos. "Besides, I don't think London's had anything this interesting since the Olympics. And that wasn't even political."

Shanice raised an eyebrow but said nothing more. She wasn't convinced, but even she couldn't deny the momentum Callie had already built. Social media was buzzing with viral clips of the bus rolling through the streets, and journalists were starting to notice. She'd already been contacted by a couple of radio stations and local publications asking for interviews. If nothing else, Callie was definitely getting attention.

She knew that Shanice was of the old school, millennial mindset, where radio was about smooth, professional broadcasting and not chaotic stunts. Shanice didn't get it. But Callie didn't care. She wasn't here for the same old boring politics and dull radio schedules. She was here to shake things up, and so far, it was working.

The clock was ticking down, and Callie could feel the buzz building in the studio. Her social media notifications were pinging non-stop, and her team was scrambling to get everything ready. It was go time.

"Okay, five minutes to air," Shanice said, adjusting her headphones and glancing at the clock. "You sure you're ready for this? It's not like you can just undo it if things go south."

Callie smirked, tapping her fingers on the desk. "You know me, Shan. I don't do anything half-arsed."

As the countdown to the show began, Callie took a deep breath and stared at the monitors. This was her moment to make her official announcement. She wasn't going to do it quietly—no, this was going to be loud, unapologetic, and full of chaos.

"That's what I'm afraid of," Shanice muttered. "Have you recorded your split links?"

Split links, Callie knew, were where the live broadcast for multiple stations had localised versions of the show, breaking up the feed for each region with localised content while keeping the main show intact. Usually used on the network shows on Bauer's Hits Network and Manic's CHR, or Vibes, network, the hosts usually recorded segments that made an illusion of local engagement for listeners across the many different areas, while doing generic links for the main network part of the show. It was a technicality, but it kept the listeners feeling like they were hearing something special for their region.

As a host of the Manic Radio Essex drive show, she'd never needed to worry about split links, and so the thought of doing London specific splits for this afternoon's show had Callie feeling a mix of excitement and a bit of dread. She'd been used to working with one regional feed, where things felt easy and straightforward. But now, with the pressure of four stations, plus her own show, relying on her to keep it fluid, sharp, and engaging, she was stepping into unknown territory. The nerves had to be pushed down—there was no room for hesitation.

"Erm... I've not got my hot keys set up as... I kinda forgot?" she said, looking at Shanice with a mischievous grin, her fingers poised over the desk.

"You stupid, stupid girl," Shanice muttered, shaking her head. "Get your arse into Studio 2, grab a producer, and get the split links done. The script is on the Sharepoint, so you should be good to go once you've got it sorted. Honestly, have you never heard of brand guidelines and required split link protocols?" Shanice added, rolling her eyes, though there was a hint of amusement in her voice.

Callie raised her hands in mock surrender. "Relax, Shan, I'll be fine. I've got this. It's not like we're broadcasting a coronation, yeah?"

"And if you shatter the illusion. We're covering three other duos, and we've got different WhatsApp numbers, different web addresses, and different localness links we have to mention for the weekend, so everything needs to be spot on. I've got my hotkeys set up, but you need to get your links recorded and sorted," Shanice finished, her voice tinged with an exasperated but fond tone. "Hurry up, before you give me an aneurysm."

* _ * _ * _ *

"And in local London news," Shanice heard on the London feeds, as she was logged into her usual East London Hits setup for the soundcheck, "The Excel arena is expected to be busy this week as the Disney 100 exhibition concludes on Monday. The exhibition, celebrating the 100th anniversary of Disney, is expected to bring in record crowds over the weekend, with many of the attractions already sold out. The family-friendly exhibition has been a huge hit this year, drawing visitors from across the UK. So, if you're looking for something to do this weekend, it's definitely worth checking out—though you might want to leave your T-shirt with Mickey on at home!"

Shanice looked up from her screen, half listening as the producer confirmed their soundcheck was good. The room felt charged, as if everyone knew something was coming. The tension was almost palpable, and it was clear the next 3 hours with Callie were going to be a drag, especially if she hadn't gotten her hotkeys, which allowed her to say one thing on one feed, but sent out a completely different short link, and the pre-recorded splits that get loaded into Zetta, which were for longer form split links on the different local feeds.

As Shanice waited for the official cue, she knew that the first seven minutes would be a sweeper, then a Spice Girls throwback track, then a Dua Lipa track in order to set the tone before Callie made her big announcement. It was the standard clock on the Manic Vibes network of locally named heritage brands and Manic Radio branded stations for this slot, depending on if there was a promo for the weekly mega networked competition. This week, the slot for the network competitions was for reminders to air at quarter past the hour, which was designed to keep the listeners' attention locked in before the big announcement. Shanice could feel the weight of the moment pressing down. The clock was ticking, and Callie, who'd always thrived on chaos, was now at the centre of it all. If she managed to pull this off—make the chaos work in her favour—it would be one for the history books.

She knew it would take at least 20 minutes for Callie, if she rushed it, or half an hour if she stayed true to her usual flair for creating a scene, to record the split links, and as it was 4 o'clock precisely, so the tension in the studio reached its peak. That meant that Shanice was covering the first half hour solo.

The Zetta and GSelector screens showed that the news and traffic were finishing, meaning that the split links she had recorded for London Vibes, North London Vibes and South London Vibes, announcing that she was covering their local hosts, would air, leaving her to concentrate on introducing her own East London Hits introduction, as she, along with her normal co-host, Gabriel Gold, would do that specific drive show.

Turning her microphone on, she nodded to the producer, her own regular producer on East London Hits drivetime, Adam Parkinson, signalling that she was ready, while Callie was elsewhere doing her split links. Shanice could feel the pulse of the station running through her veins, and she knew she had to nail this moment, especially with all the chaos unfolding on the other side of the studio. It wasn't the calm, well-oiled machine she'd been used to, but this was Manic, and nothing was ever calm here.

As she stared at the monitor, counting down the seconds until she was on air, she couldn't help but shake her head slightly. Callie had her own way of doing things, and it was always a ride. Shanice just hoped the listeners would be ready for the chaos.

"Alright fam, it's your gal, Shanice, here on East London Hits. Gabes is off today, so I'll be having a special guest on the show, some geezer from our sister station, Manic Radio Essex, who'll be joining me in a bit. Anyway, here's a bit of Spice Girls, with 2 Before 1," she said, knowing that on the South London Vibes feed, her prerecorded line of "Alright, Safh London, it's Shanice here, live and across Wimbledon, Croydon and Brixton, in for Dani and Lila, and joining me is my bestie, Callie," would be kicking off the feed for that area, a similar line saying that she was in for "Rich and Jordan", and for the pan-London station, she was in for "Kez and Harper," all using similar lines linking the Spice Girls, which Zetta would automatically playout thanks to the Speke master clock, before blending into the Dua Lipa track that would carry them through the next segment. Shanice leaned back in her chair, headphones snug, monitoring the feeds, watching the split link timestamps flash green as each one successfully fired across the four London stations and the Essex station.

Unlike some of the other CHR hosts on the Manic network, Shanice was one of those who preferred that her prep was done by herself, on paper, so she could see what she was doing before going on air, that if she had to do split links, she would do them methodically, with precision. But, with Callie's last-minute adjustments, the pressure of managing four feeds had been... less than ideal. Shanice had it all under control for now—well, mostly. She glanced at the clock once more, counting down the seconds until Callie took over and made her announcement.

Watching the counters, she noticed that the transitions between tracks would be coming up in a minute, with the master feed from Speke automatically transferring to the next track.

*_*_*_*

"I'm ready!" Callie said, walking back into Studio 1 half an hour later, knowing that she'd done a rush job in order to get the split links recorded, hoping that a technician would have sorted out the final details. She could feel the energy in the room change the moment she walked in. The team, while mildly stressed, knew something big was about to happen. The Battle Bus outside was still being tagged in every social media post, and the buzz had only amplified with each passing minute.

"Finally, you're back," Shanice muttered, adjusting her headset. "Thought you'd gotten lost in the chaos of London traffic—or worse, spray-painting the Queen's face on the side of the bus." She shot Callie a pointed look, though there was a hint of amusement in her voice.

Callie flashed her a cheeky grin. "Nah, didn't want to get too carried away. But hey, it's official now. I've got my links sorted, and the chaos is about to begin."

Shanice nodded, giving Callie a half-smile. "This better be worth it, mate. The listeners are in for a ride."

With one last check on her producer's desk, Callie settled into the chair, ready to take control. The clock ticked closer to the big announcement. It was showtime.

"Alright, East London, South London, North London, and all you Essex folk tuning in... it's time for something a little bit different," Callie's voice rang out, loud and confident, perfectly tailored for the chaos of her new political campaign. "This is Callie Hall, and I've got a little announcement for you all."

The feed, which had been playing a mix of the usual upbeat tracks, shifted in tone. The airwaves filled with anticipation as the split links cut away, leaving only Callie's voice to carry the weight of her bold declaration.

"Now, I know what you're thinking. 'Who is this? And why is she shouting at us through our speakers?' Well, I'll tell you why. Because I'm here to shake things up. I'm here to make some noise. And yes, you guessed it—I'm running for Mayor of London. That's right, folks. ME."

There was a beat of silence before the chaos erupted through the four networks. Tweets, Instagram stories, and text messages from listeners flooded in. Callie could almost hear the confusion and excitement seeping into every corner of London, each part of the city gearing up for whatever she was about to say next.

"Now, you might be wondering, why me? Why not one of those boring politicians with their well-prepared speeches and their safe policies? Well, let me tell you something, London. Politics is broken. It's been broken for years. So why not have a bit of fun with it? Why not have someone who's actually living in the city, struggling with the same stuff you all are? Transport's a nightmare. The Mayor's been in charge for ages, and what's actually changed? Exactly. Nothing. So I'm here to break that cycle. And to do that, I'm launching the Manic Collective. Forget your usual political parties; let's get loud, let's get messy, and let's show London we've had enough of the same old crap."

She paused, letting the silence hang for a moment, before slapping down the next point.

"And I know what you're thinking, 'What's the catch?' Well, the catch is simple: My first policy is to ban Capital FM. That's right, people—ban it. You've all heard the same ten songs on loop for too long, and frankly, I'm done with it. We deserve better. We deserve something that isn't just polished corporate nonsense. We deserve radio that represents the chaos, the fun, the energy of this city. Manic's better, innit!"

The buzz across social media hit a fever pitch. The chatrooms were ablaze with comments from listeners. #MakeLondonManic trended instantly. People were shocked, some amused, others outraged. But one thing was for sure: Callie Hall had their attention.

"Now, let's be real," she continued, her voice cutting through the noise. "To do it, I need nominations, I need lots of upstanding people from the London Boroughs to sign a form in March to say that I'm a fine, respectable woman, and that I'm worthy of running for Mayor. But here's the twist: you're going to sign not because I'm some great politician—I'm not. But because we're going to show the system that it can be done differently. We're going to show that the same old politics doesn't have to win. And if you don't like it, well, that's too bad. I'm still going to be here, making noise, and making sure everyone knows that you're fed up with the same old nonsense."

Callie leaned back, feeling the buzz fill the studio. She could hear Shanice's nervous chuckle behind her and the muted sounds of producers scrambling in the background. It was the moment they'd all been waiting for, the moment Callie had been preparing for. And despite everything—despite the chaos, the uncertainty, the ridiculousness of it all—she felt a rush of exhilaration. She was in control, and London was listening.

"So, there you have it, London," Callie finished, her voice turning playful. "This is my promise: a Mayor who's not afraid to cause a bit of a ruckus. A Mayor who's not afraid to say, 'Enough is enough.' If you're with me, let's make some noise, let's make a stand, and let's make London MANIC! Not just a city of red buses, high-rises, and overpriced lattes. No. A city where the chaos is celebrated, where the people actually have a voice—and we're not afraid to shout about it. Oh, you must be 18 or older, and for everyone who signs the nomination form, I'll give them a free bottle of WKD Blue as a thanks."

****

CHAPTER 4 – Registration
Monday 22nd January 2024

Callie knew that there was one important thing she needed to do, as she was planning to stand not as an independent candidate, but under the banner of a newly-formed political party. The problem was that the paperwork was a bloody nightmare. The idea of doing things "properly" felt like anathema to everything she stood for, but the legalities of getting a political party registered were non-negotiable.

Thankfully, however, the Head of Legal for Lite Group, the name that Manic had adopted in the takeover in 2022 of the original Lite Group, had a reputation for being both terrifyingly efficient and surprisingly understanding when it came to navigating the bureaucratic nightmare of political registration, as he had been part of the creation of several, albeit failed, parties that had stood for only one election and then dissolved due to lack of funding or sheer lack of public interest. Despite the failure rate, he had been well-versed in the ins and outs of election law, and if Callie was going to get anywhere, she'd need his expertise.

Sitting at a large wooden table in one of the back rooms of the Manic HQ, Callie couldn't help but feel the weight of the task in front of her. The thick stack of forms seemed almost comically daunting. She had spent the weekend touring around various boroughs in the Battle Bus, handing out flyers, shouting over the music, and promoting her bizarrely brilliant political agenda on social media. Now it was time to make it official. She had to follow the rules, even if the rules seemed designed to make anyone with a sense of chaos want to tear their hair out.

"Right, Callie," Robert Hollis, the Head of Legal for the Group and who Callie had asked to be the Nominating Officer for her campaign, said as he adjusted his glasses, eyeing the paperwork with a mixture of resigned dread and professional focus. "You're going to need to get at least 330 valid nominations from the 32 London boroughs. That's ten signatures from each borough, and they need to be from eligible voters. No funny business, no loopholes. It's all in the fine print, and believe me, the last thing we need is for this to get tangled up in a legal challenge."

Callie leaned back in her chair, rubbing her temples. This was the part she had been dreading—the moment when the chaos would have to bend to the cold, sterile reality of bureaucracy. The Battle Bus, the spray-painted slogans, the social media circus—it was all fun and games. But now? Now she was entering the land of legal jargon, forms, and procedures. The world of grown-ups.

"First, we need to know, are you going to use the post box downstairs in Reception, or your Romford home as the Party headquarters and registered address?" Robert asked, already scribbling on one of the forms with a black fountain pen that looked as though it had witnessed the fall of empires.

Callie blinked. "Wait, you're telling me I could list my flat in Romford as HQ for a political party? What, so I'd have the same legal standing as the Lib Dems but with less furniture?"

Robert didn't look up. "If you like, yes. But remember, that address will be public. Every time someone Googles the party, they'll find it. Might make for some interesting post. As Banks has told us to support you by providing whatever resources that that don't breach broadcast impartiality rules, I'd suggest using the Stratford studio building's post box as the official HQ. It's neutral, nondescript, and not full of WKD bottles and takeaway receipts."

Callie rolled her eyes. "Wow. Rude. My flat's very tidy. Mostly. But yeah, Stratford it is. At least if someone tries to egg the office, they'll hit the security gate."

Robert nodded, efficiently noting the address. "Right. Name of the party?"

Callie grinned. "The Manic Collective. Obviously."

Dennis Drummond, the Group Finance Director of Manic and the person who'd been asked by Callie to be the Treasurer, as he had an accounting degree and was a chartered accountant by profession, was already scrolling through a spreadsheet on his tablet, clearly trying not to sigh too loudly.

"If we're calling it The Manic Collective, we'll need to make sure that's not already registered or conflicting with anything that sounds remotely like a cult or a DJ collective from Shoreditch," he said, without looking up. "Also, HMRC will need a bank account linked to this name. So once you've signed the constitution, we'll need to get it set up with the accountants and then register that for the party's official financial reporting."

Callie blinked. "Wait—constitution?"

Robert, still writing, didn't even bother suppressing his smile. "Yes. All parties need a constitution. It's in the Electoral Commission guidelines. You don't need to go full Magna Carta, but you need something that outlines the aims of the party, how you elect officers, what happens if you dissolve, and so on."

Callie looked genuinely betrayed. "So I can't just write, 'Our mission is to troll London into caring about local politics again' and if that fails then just stand wherever Farage or Rishi decides to stand next, wearing a bin bag and shouting 'Vote for Chaos'?"

Robert raised an eyebrow. "You can, but I wouldn't advise it. The Electoral Commission has a surprisingly low tolerance for satire in official paperwork."

Dennis added, dryly, "And HMRC definitely doesn't. If you try to expense spray paint and WKD Blue under 'strategic campaign tools', we'll be getting audited by Wednesday."

Callie sighed, dramatically flopping forward onto the desk. "This is so not the fun part of the revolution."

"You started this circus," Robert reminded her, passing over a draft constitution that had clearly been recycled from some other short-lived political misadventure. "I've taken the liberty of preparing a template. You'll need to fill in the bits about campaign aims, party discipline—yes, discipline—and media handling."

"Media handling?" Callie sat back up, eyes narrowed. "Is that a section where I write 'post memes until they cry'?"

Robert didn't answer. He simply slid a pen across the table.

Callie took it with a groan. "Fine. But I'm adding a clause that allows me to declare raves of national significance. That counts as cultural outreach, yeah?"

"Of course it does," Robert said, without missing a beat. "Just make sure you phrase it like, 'The Party shall, from time to time, engage with the public through spontaneous civic engagement events, with amplified music and community dance participation'."

Dennis looked up from his tablet with a snort. "Honestly, that's still less vague than anything in the Labour manifesto."

Callie grinned, already scribbling notes onto the template constitution with barely-contained glee. "Right. Clause 4: The right to hold public sonic gatherings in defiance of municipal beige-ness."

Robert didn't even blink. "Clause 5 better include a statement about promoting inclusivity, responsible use of public spaces, and not physically ramming the Battle Bus into the front of Capital's HQ."

"I mean, that's not off the table," Callie muttered. "I can still park it on a weekend outside either Golden Square or Leicester Square and do gigs from the top deck, right?"

She noticed Robert's face drop at the mention of Leicester Square, and she knew why. Global Media's Head of Legal, James Jenkins KC, the same lawyer who, in 2019, forced an injunction against Manic's then branded Pepsi Chart Christmas Show that had broadcast outside the that had broadcast outside the Global HQ in Leicester Square, was still very much active in the legal world. The then CEO, Dr Scott Bennett, had survived the fallout of the so-called "Pepsi Chart Massacre", even though LBC, within 5 minutes of the Police shutting down Nelly Vixen's broadcast, had spun it into a sanctimonious sermon about public order and journalistic integrity. Callie remembered watching it all unfold while still in sixth form, the moment that first made her think radio could be more than just playlists and travel bulletins. It could be rebellion.

Robert, however, looked as though he was experiencing a very different kind of flashback.

"I'll remind you," he said with the weary patience of a man who had buried more than one legal grenade in his time, "that the injunction from the Pepsi incident is technically still on the books. If you set up a sound system within fifty metres of Global's HQ, you'll trigger enough legal alarms to light up the Thames."

"Unless," Dennis chimed in, "we get Westminster to grant us a block permit to hold a community engagement event tied to a registered political campaign. Like when you,

Rob, were part of the creation of that Traffic Wardens for Justice party in Reddish."

Callie's eyes lit up. "Oh my God, that was you? The Traffic Wardens for Justice lot? With the protest flashmob outside Aldi where everyone ticketed their own car and then demanded it be towed?"

Robert nodded solemnly. "And got ten thousand views on YouTube before it was taken down for 'vehicular self-harm'. Not my proudest moment. But the paperwork was solid."

Callie beamed. "You are so wasted on litigation. You should be writing this campaign with me. Or at least co-authoring the chaos."

Robert slid another sheet her way. "Let's survive registration first. This is the form to register your emblem and party description. You'll need a description, something that can be put on the ballot forms along with the Party name and emblem. The guidance states 'you may register up to 12 descriptions with the Commission. The rules for descriptions are the same as those for names. You do not have to register any descriptions, but if you do not your candidates can only stand under a description that is the exact registered name of the party. Each of the party's officers mentioned in section 2 must sign the application. Descriptions for parties registered to contest elections in Wales can be in English or Welsh. There is no need to provide a translation, but if a translation to or from Welsh is provided, both the Welsh and the English versions will be jointly registered as the description. Where both an English and Welsh version of a description are given, this counts as a single description against the 12 descriptions limit.'"

Callie squinted down at the form as Robert droned on, her brain latching onto the one part that truly mattered.

"Wait... so I can have twelve different ballot descriptions? Like, legally?" she asked, her eyes widening.

Robert nodded, grim as ever. "Yes, and I suggest you use all twelve strategically. You can have different slogans or straplines appear next to your name on the ballot paper, depending on the ward or area, so long as they're pre-registered. But they must all be signed off by you, me, and Dennis."

Callie rubbed her hands together like a cartoon villain. "Oh, this is going to be delicious."

Dennis looked up from his spreadsheet, clearly already regretting his involvement. "Please tell me we're not going to have to defend 'Callie Hall – Chaos But Make It Legal' in front of the Electoral Commission."

Callie pointed a finger at him. "Actually, that's not bad. Write that one down."

Robert sighed but dutifully added it to a growing list.

"Alright," he muttered. "Let's brainstorm. We'll need a proper mix—some that sound vaguely legit, some that will catch the eye, and some that will make people think they've gone mad."

"Sorted," Callie said, grabbing a fresh sheet of paper. "How about:

1. *The Manic Collective – Make London Fun Again*

2. *Callie Hall – Chaos With a Soundtrack*

3. *Vote Callie – Free WKD and No Boring Radio*

4. *The Manic Collective – No More Beige Politics*

5. *Callie Hall – Too Loud To Ignore*

6. *The Manic Collective – Radio But Make It Policy*

7. *Callie Hall – Like Boris But With Better Playlists*

8. *The Manic Collective – Vibes Over Vested Interests*

9. *Callie Hall – Because You're Bored of Everyone Else*

10. *The Manic Collective – For Those Who've Stopped Believing*

11. *Callie Hall – Probably Not The Worst Option*

12. *The Manic Collective – This Is A Protest Vote, Right?"*

Dennis stared at her. "You're genuinely going to submit that last one?"

Callie grinned. "Mate, if you've ever met a London voter, you know that might actually win me Croydon."

Robert shook his head, shoulders slumping. "Fine. But make sure the wording matches exactly when we submit. If it's even a comma off, the Commission will bounce it."

"Now, I've... well, got a friend, he's a minor TOWIE cast member, and he's willing to be my celebrity endorser for the socials," Callie said with a smirk that suggested she already knew how ridiculous it sounded. "He was in two episodes and got pied off in Sugar Hut, but he's got, like, 18k followers and a discount code for teeth whitening kits."

Dennis groaned audibly, rubbing his temples. "We're building a political party, Callie. Not a group chat for people who peaked at a Basildon nightclub."

Robert, however, barely blinked. "That's fine, but make sure any endorsements are disclosed appropriately under the Electoral Commission's rules. They'll need to be clearly labelled as paid or unpaid promotion depending on the arrangement. And for the love of God, don't have him do a TikTok in front of a polling station."

Callie pulled a face. "You're no fun."

"I'm still fun," Robert said, deadpan. "I just don't want to spend the rest of the year explaining to a judge why one of our campaign materials included a giveaway for lip fillers and a QR code that linked to a Spotify playlist titled Vote For Me Or I'll Cry."

Dennis, flicking through a spreadsheet labelled Projected Budget - Manic Collective Mayoral Campaign, raised an eyebrow. "Speaking of which, where exactly is the money coming from for this mess?"

Callie shrugged. "Banks sorted a fund. Said I've got £200k to play with as long as I don't get Ofcom'd."

Robert raised a hand like a strict schoolteacher. "You will get Ofcom'd if you mention it on air during programming. You are now a registered political entity. You must be impartial during any on-air appearances that are not clearly declared as campaign segments. I would recommend stepping down from your show during the campaign, but I have a feeling you won't, as you're as you're constitutionally incapable of staying quiet for more than 15 seconds," he finished, without looking up from the form he was now cross-referencing against Electoral Commission compliance guidance.

Callie smirked. "Rude, but not wrong."

Dennis sighed and leaned back in his chair, fixing her with a look of weary exasperation. "Let me guess, you're going to 'walk the line' and try and blur the boundaries of what's technically 'editorial content' versus 'campaigning', aren't you?"

"Mate, I *am* editorial content," Callie replied with a grin, snapping a picture of the mess of forms in front of her and immediately posting it to her campaign's Instagram with the caption:

@calliehall4ldn: 📷 *Signing my soul away for bureaucracy and vibes. #MakeLondonManic #PaperworkIsPunk*

The Instagram post was barely five minutes old before the notifications started flying in. Callie watched the likes rack up, a steady stream of blue thumbs, heart-eyes, and laughing-crying emojis. Someone had already commented: *"Is that a WHSmith pen you're signing London's fate with?"*

Robert didn't look up. "You realise the Electoral Commission reviews social media too, yes?"

"Cool," Callie replied. "They can like, comment and subscribe."

Dennis pinched the bridge of his nose and muttered, "We're going to get sanctioned by lunchtime."

"Right, Callie, last bit. Do you have a logo, or is the Graphics Team creating an emblem for you?" Robert asked, tapping the section of the form that read "Party Emblem (must be in JPEG or PNG format, no larger than 1MB, and suitable for black-and-white printing)" with a finger that looked like it had pointed at one too many cease-and-desist letters.

Callie blinked. "Oh yeah. They're resketching the Manic logo to look as if it were graffitied on a toilet wall in Camden. Proper punk vibes. Neon lightning bolt through a radio tower, scuffed lettering, bit of stencil spray effect—y'know, like Banksy if he was raised on WKD and TikTok."

Robert raised an eyebrow. "And you're confident it meets the Electoral Commission's guidance on 'not resembling a weapon, a royal insignia, or containing offensive imagery'?"

"It's a lightning bolt," Callie said innocently. "Not a knife. Unless you squint."

Dennis groaned again. "Why does every meeting with you feel like I'm in a fever dream produced by Channel 4?"

Callie grinned. "Because I'm a disruptor, babes."

There was a knock on the door. A young intern in a Manic Radio fleece poked her head in, holding a USB stick.

"Sorry to interrupt—Callie, Graphics just sent over three drafts of the emblem. They want you to pick one so they can finalise it for the Electoral Commission upload. And they said—'tell her to stop cropping it into Instagram stories before it's approved'. Also… there's a version with a pigeon wearing headphones if you're feeling brave."

Callie's eyes lit up. "Send me that one. Pigeons are the true Londoners."

Callie grinned at the intern like she'd just been handed a rare vinyl by Dave Grohl himself. "Absolutely yes to the pigeon. That's the one. It's got strong Trafalgar Square energy."

Robert didn't even bother looking up. "As long as the pigeon isn't flipping the bird or defecating on a ballot box, I suppose it passes."

Dennis tapped his tablet, loading up the emblem options via the internal SharePoint. "Option one is the classic tower-and-bolt. Option two is the one with dripping neon graffiti-style text. Option three…" He stopped, eyebrows raised, "…has a pigeon in sunglasses DJing on a vinyl deck made of oyster cards."

Callie beamed. "Option three. Lock it in."

Robert cleared his throat. "You realise this is going to be printed next to your name on the actual mayoral ballot, right? That pigeon is going to be immortalised in British political history."

"That's the dream, Rob," Callie said, leaning back in her chair with all the smugness of someone who knew she was about to go viral again. "That's the legacy."

The intern handed over the USB, gave a cautious thumbs-up, and backed out of the room like she'd just witnessed state secrets being traded for WKD and chaos.

Dennis, meanwhile, opened a folder titled "Compliance & Risk: Manic Collective" and sighed like a man watching a puppy try to drive a Ferrari. "Callie, we still need to file the list of campaign agents, your proposed schedule of expenses, and—oh god—your slogan compliance forms."

"I've got slogans for days, babe," Callie said, pulling a crumpled notepad from her oversized hoodie. "Look, here—'Make the DLR Sexy Again', 'Sadiq Who?', and my personal favourite: 'If You're Reading This, Vote For Me.'"

Robert, miraculously, still hadn't murdered her. "And your plan for filing spending reports?"

"I'll send Dennis my Monzo statements every week and he can yell at me when I buy something stupid," she said sweetly.

"I already hate this," Dennis muttered, dragging the budget tracker into a separate window labelled 'Disaster Plan'.

Just then, Jordan strolled into the room with two flat whites and a can of Red Bull precariously balanced on top. "Alright, paperwork warriors. How's the revolution coming along? Got your pigeon locked in?"

Callie grabbed the Red Bull, cracked it open like it was champagne, and nodded. "We are now an official party with a DJ pigeon as our emblem and twelve ballot descriptions that range from mildly ironic to full-on 'burn the system' energy."

Jordan raised a brow. "You remembered to submit the 'Free WKD' one, right?"

"Obviously," Callie replied, sipping the drink with a victorious glint in her eye. "Now all we need is 330 sane-ish people across London willing to sign a form declaring I'm legally acceptable to run for office."

Dennis groaned. "Which reminds me—we need to start drafting borough-specific outreach. The form needs ten valid voters per borough. We've got until March. So unless you've got an army of TikTokers with clipboards…"

Callie's grin widened. "Oh, we've got something better."

****

CHAPTER 5 – Media Circus
Tuesday 23rd January 2024

Callie knew that the Daily Mail would have something to say about her posting her application form to register The Manic Collective as a political party with the caption: *"Signing my soul away for bureaucracy and vibes. #MakeLondonManic #PaperworkIsPunk"* on her Instagram, X, and TikTok.

She wasn't wrong.

By 9:00am, the headline was live on MailOnline:

"EXCLUSIVE: Radio DJ Turns 'Joke' Politician – Calls Bureaucracy 'Punk' as She Vows to BAN Capital FM

Callie Hall, 21, branded 'unhinged' and 'dangerous' after launching bizarre bid to run for Mayor of London… supported by £200,000 from 'mystery media backers'.

By Saddam Bashir, Media Editor for Mail Online"

Callie knew from her conversations with Nelly Vixen, the host of Manic's O2 Top 40 on Sundays, that the Mail's media team practically lived on X, had burner TikTok accounts, and probably a WhatsApp group chat named " SPICE LEVEL 100: Radio Chaos". She also knew Nelly had been at University in Worcester, a town in the Midlands more known for its sauce than its student journalism, with Bashir, and that she had once been the subject of her own MailOnline hit piece "SHOCK JOCK SHAME – OFCOM PROBES DR NELLY VIXEN

AFTER RADIO RANT", after she had used the words "mentally retarded" and "spastic" on a 2019 episode of the then titled UK40Chart, prior to the Pepsi and Gazprom sponsorship of the show, and had been rewarded with nothing but support from then CEO, Dr Scott Bennett, as she had got a 30% increase in listeners who would tune in to see what unscripted chaos might come next.

"According to the Instagram post, which was uploaded from the Stratford studios of Manic Radio, Ms Hall posed with a can of Red Bull, a pile of papers, and what appears to be a doodle of a pigeon wearing headphones—believed to be her party's emblem. Sources close to Hall claim the bird 'represents London's scrappy spirit', while critics argue it's 'everything wrong with Gen Z politics'.

Head of Legal for Global Media and Entertainment, James Jenkins KC, stated that "Media personalities who stand for public office, such as Ms Hall, are required by OFCOM to stand down from their shows as soon as the Notice of Election is published by the relevant Returning Officer. Any attempt to campaign while on air could amount to a serious breach of broadcast impartiality rules.

"Furthermore, Ms Hall, as an employee of Manic Radio, is legally responsible for continuing her actions on both regulated platforms and social media, and we expect the Electoral Commission and OFCOM to scrutinise this campaign closely."

The MailOnline has asked OFCOM, the Greater London Authority and the Electoral Commission for a statement, the latter of which provided the following:

"The election for the Mayor of London has not yet been formally called. We can confirm that no individuals are currently considered candidates under election law. As such, while individuals may announce intentions, formal campaigning rules including broadcast impartiality and expenditure regulations come into effect only once the Notice of Election has been published by the Greater London Returning Officer."

Thomas Brown, an expert in media regulation and political law at the London School of Economics, was quoted as saying "Callie Hall's campaign is testing the limits of election law in a digital-first age. What we're seeing is an intentional blurring of the lines between satire, influencer culture, and political mobilisation. Whether it's legally compliant will depend entirely on timing—but it's certainly disruptive.""

Callie noticed, while sitting in her Romford flat, that she had also qualified for the 'Sidebar of Shame', a feature in the Mail's Online edition which was normally reserved for Love Island contestants, disgraced Tory councillors, or B-list actresses leaving Soho House in see-through leggings.

Her entry sat comfortably between a blurry shot of a soap star's "nip slip horror" and an exposé on a former Strictly contestant's "secret heartbreak". Her photo, complete with DJ Pigeon in the background and her signature neon hoodie that read *RAVE FIRST, VOTE LATER*, had been captioned ***"WHO IS CALLIE HALL: MANIC RADIO ESSEX'S RABBLE ROUSER"***.

Reading the sidebar article, she had to laugh.

"A graduate of the University of Essex and former Kiss Fresh early Breakfast presenter, Callie's bursting onto the radio scene in May 2023 was not the usual slow-burn affair common to aspiring DJs. Upon joining Bauer's Kiss Fresh brand, Hall caused controversy when she called their "Cash Register" network promotion 'corporate thottery for rent arrears' live on air. Although her contract wasn't renewed after that incident, it was reportedly this outburst that brought her to the attention of Manic Radio's talent scouts, who were actively seeking irreverent voices for their local contemporary hit brands.

A born Romford native, Hall wears her hometown like a badge of honour—and a punchline. She has described herself in interviews as 'Romford's answer to Rage Against the Machine, but with more glitter and worse GCSEs'. With her signature mix of brutal honesty, political irreverence and influencer-style visuals, Hall's mayoral bid is raising eyebrows across the capital's media and political elite."

Callie, scrolling with her feet up on the arm of her sofa and a stale Yazoo bottle on the floor beside her, wasn't sure whether to be insulted or deeply, perversely flattered. Her inbox was already flooding with interview requests: BBC Breakfast, Newsnight, LBC, even Steph's Packed Lunch—which she thought had been cancelled, but apparently was still staggering on in some Channel 4 side-room like a zombie game show for mums on maternity leave.

She was still in her dressing gown when London Vibes drive host Keegan "Kez" Mahoney rang her mobile, his voice crackling through the line like someone was trying to tune a pirate frequency using a fork and a radiator.

"Callie, babe. You're leading the trending tab on TikTok, three of your slogans have already been ripped for bootleg T-shirts, and Jenkins KC just went full Churchill on LBC. He's doing a cover show, in for Nick Ferrari. Called your campaign 'a stain on public discourse' and said—and I quote—'This woman wouldn't know political nuance if it bit her on the bum outside a kebab shop.' I nearly crashed my car laughing."

Callie snorted with laughter, grinning. "Might ring in then, see if I can get a chat with him on air, see if he can handle the heat without hiding behind his silk robes and a producer with the dump button."

* _ * _ * _ *

James Jenkins KC, temporarily filling in for Nick Ferrari on LBC, looked like a man trying to finish his fifth espresso without screaming. Dressed in his signature charcoal three-piece suit, his tie tighter than most people's broadband connection, he surveyed the control room through the glass with steely disapproval.

A close family friend of Global Founder Ashley Tabor-King, Jenkins enjoyed these occasional appearances on air. They gave him a chance to speak directly to the masses without the filtering middlemen of legalese and court transcripts. It let him, as he liked to say, "clear up the rubbish polluting the public square." This morning, that rubbish came in the form of a 21-year-old radio DJ with a Red Bull can, a pigeon mascot, and a fluorescent hoodie who had declared herself a mayoral candidate and threatened, quite publicly, to ban Capital FM.

Which, to Jenkins, was sacrilege.

"I'm going to say it plainly," he was now intoning, lips taut and voice dipped in moral clarity, "London is not a playground for TikTok stunts and glorified radio dares. This woman—Miss Hall—is not a politician. She's an influencer with a loudspeaker. A provocateur. And in my professional opinion—speaking both as a King's Counsel and the Head of Legal for a major UK broadcaster—she is a danger to the democratic process."

In the control room, Jenkins's producer, Imran, mouthed silently to a colleague: *drama queen*.

Jenkins continued.

"Not only has she violated every unspoken tenet of political seriousness, but she's mocked the very offices of governance she claims to aspire to. Mayor of London is not a title for satire, it's not a vehicle for brand-building, and it certainly isn't a TikTok challenge you complete between oat milk lattes and ironic protest memes."

He paused, letting the weight of his disapproval settle like smog across the capital.

"Do you know what I saw this morning?" he went on, fury rising in a controlled swell. "A photograph of a woman with unbrushed hair, no shoes, sitting on a beanbag, filling in official registration paperwork with what appears to be a glitter gel pen. That's not politics. That's a parody. We are witnessing, ladies and gentlemen, the erosion of civic dignity in real time. Frank in Birmingham," he said, looking at the note his producer had just handed him, "you're on the line."

Frank, a retired police sergeant from Sutton Coldfield, came on the air, audibly wheezing with the effort of indignation.

"James, I've served this country. Thirty-two years, traffic division, West Midlands. I've seen streakers, I've seen protesters dressed as Peppa Pig, but I draw the line at that—at a pigeon on a ballot paper. My grandson asked if she was a joke candidate. I told him, 'Son, jokes don't cost £200,000.'"

Jenkins chuckled. "Quite right, Frank. Quite right. And yet the electoral system—designed for legitimate political actors—is being bent into a social media content pipeline. Callie Hall is not running for Mayor. She's auditioning for the next Netflix docuseries: How I Broke Britain in 10 Steps and a Sparkly Tracksuit. Politics, in my humble opinion, should be left to the responsible, knowledgeable and accountable. Not to be accused by the feminist lobby, I will admit that my own wife, Carly, an advisor on Diversity, Equality and Inclusion to multiple media outlets, from Global Media to a certain German owned media conglomerate —"

He heard Imran cough the word Bauer in his ear, and raised a brow—

"—yes, a certain German-owned conglomerate—agrees with me. What we need is reform, not rave culture posing as revolution."

Imran tapped his pen against the glass with the intensity of someone trying to signal a nuclear detonation. The next caller was already queued. A young woman from Tooting, who had been listening via the LBC app while queueing at a Pret, was up next. Jenkins glanced at her details: "Millie, 23, student nurse."

He nodded for the line to be opened.

"Millie, go ahead."

"Hi James," came the voice, bright, slightly nervous, crackling slightly over mobile. "Um, no offence, but you sound like my uncle before he's had his morning coffee. Callie Hall might not be the usual sort of politician, but I think that's the point. Like, the fact you're this angry means she's doing something right."

Jenkins exhaled slowly. "Doing something right? By trivialising civic office? By offering alcohol in exchange for nominations?"

Millie giggled. "Honestly? Yeah. I'm tired of the same old faces pretending they care. At least she's not pretending. And if she wants to DJ on a battle bus with a pigeon on her ballot, well—maybe that's exactly what London needs."

"Millie, with all due respect, I think you're missing the point," Jenkins replied, his tone still tight. "What London needs is leadership. Not social media stunts or 'vibe' politics. This is a city of over 8 million people. We deserve someone who's got a deep understanding of governance, not just an understanding of TikTok algorithms and how to create viral content."

He paused for a moment, trying to regain control of the narrative. "You see, this kind of spectacle just undermines the seriousness of our political system. Politics isn't about flashy logos or memes. It's about working through the issues that matter—transport, housing, policing, and education. It's about providing real solutions, not just doing the latest thing that gets you likes."

Millie laughed again, but it wasn't the kind of laugh Jenkins was expecting. It was a relaxed, knowing laugh that made him pause. "Yeah, I get that. But have you seen the state of the last few mayors? They've all been polished, well-spoken and 'serious'—but they're all about the same things, aren't they? Sadiq Khan's been mayor for ages, and look at the state of transport, housing prices, and air pollution. Everyone's so busy playing the game that they forget about the people at the bottom who need to see a change. I'm not saying Callie's the answer to everything, but at least she's doing something different. She's loud, yeah, and maybe a bit chaotic, but we need that. Look at what she's getting done—she's shaking things up."

Jenkins's face contorted in frustration, but he tried to remain calm. "So, you think that we should vote for someone who's completely unqualified and simply here to make noise? Is that what you're saying, Millie?"

Millie didn't hesitate. "Honestly, yeah. Maybe it's time we had someone who doesn't fit the mould. If Callie can't do the job, fine. But at least she's making us question the system. She's not just accepting the status quo."

Jenkins looked into the control room glass, giving Imran a long, pained look. The producer shrugged, holding up his hands as if to say, 'What do you expect?'

"Alright, Millie," Jenkins said, trying to regain some semblance of authority. "But I think you're making a dangerous mistake here. The power of leadership lies in experience and understanding. It's not a joke. It's not an Instagram story. Politics requires a level of maturity that Callie Hall simply doesn't possess."

Millie's voice softened a little, but there was still a playful edge to it. "I think Callie gets it more than you do, James. She knows people are fed up. And if she's doing it through memes and madness—maybe that's just how it needs to be done now. Who knows? Maybe we need a mayor who's as chaotic as London itself."

"Thank you for your call, Millie," Jenkins replied, now clearly struggling to hide his frustration. He gestured at Imran to take the call off-air. "That was... a lot."

Looking at his screen, he noticed his next caller was the woman herself, the chaos magnet that was Callie Hall.

Imran was grinning behind the glass. He'd let her through. Of course he had. Jenkins glared at him, mouthing "WHY?" in a manner reminiscent of a man who'd just found a rat in his teacup.

Imran just pointed at his headset and mouthed back: "She asked to come on. Said she's got a right of reply. We checked—no regs broken yet."

The LBC producer's shrug was almost apologetic. Almost.

Jenkins's jaw tightened. He didn't like being cornered. Least of all by a fluorescent twenty-one-year-old with a caffeine addiction and a pigeon logo. But this, he knew, was a moment he could use—to stamp authority on the discourse. To "frame the narrative" as his PR team would say.

With a careful breath, he leant into the mic.

"Joining us now, in what can only be described as a moment of civic irony, is Miss Callie Hall herself. Miss Hall, good morning."

Her voice came through crisp, confident and laced with mischief.

"Morning, James. Or do I have to call you KC Jenkins, head of morality for the Great British Public?"

Jenkins gave a tight-lipped smile. "Let's stick with James for now. You've certainly been busy. Would you care to explain to our listeners exactly what this is? What you're trying to achieve?"

There was a pause. Then came the unmistakable crack-hiss of a Red Bull can being opened.

"What I'm trying to achieve, James," Callie replied brightly, "is to make London politics less beige. You lot have had your turn. You've had mayors with posh educations and sharp suits who've promised the world and delivered, what? Delays on the Jubilee line and bin collections that make Tower Hamlets look like the set of I Am Legend.”

A chorus of chuckles rippled through the control room.

“I’m just saying,” she continued, “maybe it’s time we tried something new. Maybe politics doesn’t need to be all serious voices and serious ties and the occasional scandal buried under a charity photo op. Maybe what it needs is someone who understands TikTok trends and how to fill in a ballot form.”

Jenkins jumped in. “You say that as if political office is a vibe, Miss Hall. As if it’s a social experiment, not a civic duty.”

Callie didn’t flinch. “And you say that like political office hasn’t already been turned into a brand. Come on, James. We had a man ride a zipline with Union Jacks and another one trapped in a fridge to avoid questions. You don’t get to lecture me about ‘seriousness’ when the last decade has been a circus with worse makeup than mine.”

That landed.

The phone lines lit up like a Christmas tree.

Imran mouthed: “She’s good.”

Jenkins faltered, then straightened in his chair. “Let’s talk policy. You want to ban Capital FM?”

“Absolutely.”

“Why?”

"Because," she replied with a wicked grin you could hear through the airwaves, "if I hear 'Flowers' by Miley Cyrus one more time I'm going to launch myself into the Thames. That station's been playing the same ten songs for a decade. It's not a radio network, it's a Spotify ad with traffic updates."

Jenkins gave a dry chuckle. "You realise, of course, that banning a radio station isn't within the Mayor's remit? Also, I may remind you that your station is just as guilty of playing the same. Obviously, I won't mention that the Sheikh owned network you work for has lost several lawsuits in the past few years for exactly that reason. But I would imagine your legal department has you under tighter control than a preschool class on a sugar high."

Callie barked a laugh. "Oh, trust me, Rob from Legal's got me on a leash tighter than OFCOM's annual report. But here's the thing, James—do I know banning Capital is technically outside the Mayor's remit? Yes. Am I saying it anyway? Also yes. Because it's about energy. It's about taking the mick out of the bland corporate sludge that's infected everything from music to politics. People get it. It's a metaphor."

Jenkins bristled. "You think governance is a place for metaphors?"

"I think governance has been stuck using clichés for twenty years," she snapped back. "Look, this isn't about whether I can or can't legally turf out Roman Kemp and company. It's about the fact that no one believes in politics anymore. You don't fix apathy with PowerPoints and policy PDFs. You fix it by getting people to care. If that takes a fluorescent pigeon and some cheeky slogans, so be it."

There was a silence—a momentary pause that buzzed with live radio tension.

Jenkins cleared his throat. "And what, pray tell, happens if you win?"

Callie didn't hesitate.

"Then we're going to party," she said. "But the good kind. The kind where we slash TFL fares, kickstart night buses again, convert empty luxury flats into emergency housing, and yes—maybe throw a city-wide rave in Victoria Park to celebrate. I'll DJ the opening set. With the pigeon."

Imran's laugh snorted through the feed and had to be muted.

Jenkins shook his head. "This is absurd."

Callie replied, calmly, "You know what's absurd? Six hundred quid a month for a shared room in Barking with black mould and a broken boiler. You know what else? A travelcard that costs more than my rent used to. But sure, James, blame the pigeon."

Jenkins pressed the dump button quicker than a Conservative MP resigns in a WhatsApp group.

But it was too late.

The clip had already gone out across the app, recorded by listeners who were screen-grabbing, tagging, and laughing. Within minutes, "Blame the Pigeon" was trending on X, accompanied by a Photoshopped image of Callie holding a gavel in one hand and a rave whistle in the other, standing atop a CGI DJ pigeon on the roof of City Hall. The caption? *"Not all heroes wear suits. Some wear neon and hold a Bluetooth speaker."*

****

CHAPTER 6 – Confirmation
Friday 23rd February 2024

It had been a month since the forms to register The Manic Collective as a political party had been handed in, accompanied by a pigeon logo, twelve legally questionable ballot slogans, and the faint but undeniable aroma of cheap energy drinks and giddy anarchy.

As Callie Hall strutted into the Stratford Olympic Park studios of Manic Radio—her battered neon-orange puffer slung off one shoulder, clutching a caramel iced latte she'd had no business buying in February—she had a feeling. Not a premonition, exactly, but one of those twitchy twinges in the pit of her stomach that usually came before chaos. The sort of feeling she used to get before jumping a fence at a festival or submitting a wildly unfiltered voice note to air.

If she looked in her pigeon hole—her actual, physical one; a battered metal tray wedged in beside those of more respectable colleagues—it wouldn't be filled with the usual circulars or fan mail from that one listener in Chelmsford who sent her glittery postcards. No. Today, she had a hunch something else would be waiting for her.

And she was right.

There, wedged awkwardly between an unsigned birthday card from someone in HR and a flyer for a long-cancelled office yoga session, sat a thick, official-looking envelope. The kind that oozed bureaucratic smugness. White, windowed, and marked "Electoral Commission – For Addressee Only".

"Oh, bloody hell," Callie muttered, nearly dropping her latte.

Behind her, Jordan McCabe, her long-suffering producer and personal chaos sponge, emerged from the corridor with two headphones tangled around his wrist and a granola bar hanging out of his mouth like a cigar.

"Is that it?" he mumbled around the wrapper. "Is that the letter?"

"Looks like," Callie said, holding it aloft like she was about to summon a lightning bolt from it. "It's either confirmation or the politest takedown of a revolution since Ofcom gave Nelly Vixen that 'strong warning' about her 'condom chucking' stunt."

Jordan snorted. "You gonna open it or just stare at it like it's got nuclear codes inside?"

Callie turned the envelope over in her hands, then, with all the reverence of someone unboxing a limited edition vinyl, tore the top open.

It was real.

It was official.

The Manic Collective had been registered.

"Yo, Harper," she said, waving the letter above her head and marching past the open-plan desks towards Harper Prince, her counterpart on the London Vibes pan-London drive show, grinning. "Get the klaxon ready. This is not a drill."

The Stratford studios erupted the moment Harper spun around in her chair, took one look at the envelope in Callie's hand, and screamed, "No. Bloody. Way."

Harper—perpetually stylish in vintage Manic FM bomber jackets and eyeliner that could cut glass—was already scrambling for the SoundFX pad that the Manic team affectionately referred to as the "Chaos Deck." It was normally reserved for stunt links, fake airhorns, or that one sample of Cardi B saying "okurrr" that someone had forgotten to remove from the Zetta library in 2022.

She didn't hesitate. She hit the neon orange button labelled KLAXON.

From every open mic and monitor across the Stratford HQ floor, a colossal "BWAAARP-BWAARP-BWAARP" rang out—an unholy trinity of foghorn, rave siren and school fire drill. A handful of interns screamed. Someone dropped a tray of mugs. Even the cleaner pushing the hoover near Studio 3 didn't flinch—just calmly turned her machine off, nodded once in solidarity, and went back to her business.

Callie grinned. Jordan was already filming, the camera on his phone locked to her face. "Tell 'em," he whispered from behind the lens.

She held the paper aloft and shouted, "The Manic Collective is now a real party, bitches!"

A round of sarcastic cheers erupted from the East London Hits edit suite. One of the newsreaders leaned out and clapped with a dry, "What, like... legally?"

Callie grinned, waving the paperwork like a football fan brandishing a golden ticket to the World Cup Final.

"Yes. Legal as a late-night kebab and twice as messy."

Behind her, Shanice Turner appeared at the threshold of Studio 1 with a mug of green tea and her usual air of barely-contained disapproval. "Do you mind?" she deadpanned, "Some of us are trying to pre-record their Manic Dance Belters shows for tonight and tomorrow."

Callie spun on her heel with the poise of a panto villain, brandishing the letter at Shanice like it was Excalibur.

"Dance Belters can wait, Shan. Democracy is happening."

Shanice raised an eyebrow. "Oh, is that what we're calling it now?"

David Cole, the Head of PR for Manic's Olympic Park hub, and Tash Crozier, one of the Events Producers, a job which increasingly involved managing Callie's spontaneous descents into public mayhem, appeared from the kitchen area with near-synchronised sighs. They'd heard the klaxon, of course. Everyone had.

David, wearing his usual combo of Topman blazer over a Radiohead tour tee, was already palming his forehead as he walked.

"Callie," he said, in the voice of someone who'd recently had to explain to ITV's compliance team why one of their drive presenters had threatened to 'exorcise the newsreader' on air. "Tell me you haven't just announced this live."

Callie looked wounded. "David, please. I'm not an idiot."

A beat.

"Tash, dear, do you think, as the Manic Battle Bus has an OB setup, we could do my Manic Radio Essex drive show live from Lakeside, on board the bus? Do it from the bus station there, as... well, it is a bus."

Callie knew her request was a bit mad, but she also knew it was exactly the kind of stunt that would dominate TikTok for hours. The fact that Thurrock was in Essex, but close enough to London that people might mistake it for "proper political outreach" was, frankly, just icing on the rave-flavoured cake.

Tash paused, her mouth half-open with a spoon of instant porridge hovering somewhere between mug and mouth. She blinked. "You want to do the show... from the Lakeside bus station?"

Callie beamed. "Exactly. It's because Lakeside is in Essex, so I'm hosting from Essex and not here, for the afternoon, and... most commuters are coming home from London or are stuck on the M25, so it's not as if I'm not targeting those who have watercooler chats about politics at work but live in an area where WKD is sold two-for-one next to the baked beans aisle. Anyway, David, any chance you can set up a few social media accounts for the campaign as the party is now official? One for DJ Pigeon, one for the party, and one for me to troll Sadiq and whoever the Tories are running this week. I want vibe-to-vote content, innit." She finished this entire tirade in one breath, dumped her iced latte on the desk next to the

Studio 2 soundboard, and gave the letter from the Electoral Commission a theatrical little curtsy.

David exhaled through his nose like a disappointed sixth form tutor and handed over his iPad to Tash. "Start the OB request for Lakeside, God help us. I'll have to phone Legal and explain how we're now apparently broadcasting election content from a Thurrock bus depot."

"Again," Callie said brightly, "it's an Essex OB. Manic Essex. I'm not talking about the campaign live. Just vibing."

Jordan piped up from the side of the room, "The vibe is the campaign."

"Exactly!" Callie shouted, finger in the air like she'd just cracked open a philosophy A-Level essay.

Tash slumped into the production booth with the resigned grace of a woman already planning which vodka miniature she was going to nick from the events cupboard later.

*_*_*_*

@DJPigeonManic: *Coo coo, guess which party is now official #ManicInnit*

@ManicInnit: *We're the Manic Collective. We believe in vibes, value meals, and a total rework of the status quo.*

@calliehall4ldn: *I will make the DLR sexy again. That's a manifesto promise, not a threat.*

The tweet had barely been up ten minutes before DJ Pigeon's first meme dropped. A grainy close-up of the actual Electoral Commission letter, captioned in chunky Comic Sans:

@DJPigeonManic: *This doc just legalised chaos.* 🐦 🔊 *#VoteManic*

Within the hour, someone had remixed it into a TikTok sound layered over "Boom Boom Pow" by The Black Eyed Peas, autotuning Callie's phrase "Legal as a late-night kebab and twice as messy" to sound like a bass drop.

It had been an hour since Callie had walked into the studios, and there was some bad news. Lakeside had rejected her request to block off a section of the bus station for what their operations team described as "a politically ambiguous DJ set involving a costumed bird and unlicensed bubble machines." Worse still, Essex Police had called David Cole directly, asking whether Manic Radio Essex was planning a "flashmob of voters" at the Thurrock Shopping Centre and if marshals would be provided.

Callie took the news with all the maturity of a sleep-deprived teenager being told the Wi-Fi was down.

"What do you *mean* they said no?" she barked from the middle of the newsroom, one foot propped dramatically on a plastic stool and the other tapping an arrhythmic beat on the studio floor tiles.

David rubbed his temples. "Apparently, and I quote, 'a rave bus with political affiliations contravenes Lakeside's brand partnership obligations and health & safety framework.' Also, someone in security googled 'DJ Pigeon' and now thinks we're an anarchist cult."

"That's slanderous," Callie said. "We're not a cult. We're a vibes-based movement with moderately radical intentions and decent playlist curation."

Jordan was perched on a wheely chair, spinning slowly in lazy circles. "To be fair, Callie, we *do* have a mascot. And a slogan that includes the phrase 'get pissed.' It's a bit... you know... fringe party energy."

"Fringe parties don't trend on TikTok," Callie said primly, pulling out her phone and triumphantly waving it. "Over 300k views and counting. And the DJ Pigeon account's already got more followers than Reform UK's official page."

David sighed. "That is… depressingly impressive."

Tash looked up from her laptop with a wince. "Okay, so here's what I've managed. We can't do the OB from Lakeside. But… I can get Leicester Square… on Saturday 5th April 2024… hopefully. I've also booked several stop offs over the next month and half until then, at least 1 stop off in each London Borough. Oh, and David has put out on the Manic Essex socials that you're doing your Manic Radio Essex drive tonight... from the M25... from the bus... going round it."

Callie blinked. "The… M25? Like, the M25?"

Jordan, now upside down in his chair and filming content for TikTok with one hand, nodded. "Like the most cursed ring road in Britain. I mean, it's got metaphorical vibes, yeah? Just endlessly circling London, like a lost Uber driver in purgatory."

Callie stared at them both. "I'm broadcasting… drive time… from the M25."

David looked dangerously close to bursting a blood vessel. "It's the only location nobody can object to, because technically it's not a location. It's a concept. A state of mind. A bureaucratic black hole where jurisdiction goes to die. And if we don't brand this right, we're going to have the Highways Agency, Ofcom, and about six different local councils chasing us with pitchforks."

Callie lit up. "Perfect. We'll do it in a full circle. We start in Thurrock, go clockwise, finish where we began. 117 miles of banter, bangers, and bollocks. We'll call it the Manic Ring of Fire."

Tash groaned audibly. "You're going to get us all fired."

But David just nodded slowly, defeated. "I'll notify Legal."

*_*_*_*

Callie had to chuckle at the split link on the network afternoon show that had just aired, as, during the last half hour of the Kyle and Sue Afternoon Show on Manic Radio, they would do a segment which was a 30 second 'What's Ahead at Drive' part, which was pre-recorded, like most split links where different stations in the Manic network would play out the same conversation between the two afternoon hosts, Kyle Robinson and Sue

Parkinson, but localised for the different regions. Some regions, like Essex, had their own local drive, which is why Callie had one such split link, whereas stations like Derbyshire Delight, smaller markets where there was only need for a local breakfast show, carried networked content for the rest of the day.

"So, what's happening at Drive?" Kyle had asked on air, and Callie, who was listening while the setup was ongoing as the bus rolled through Plaistow on its way to the A13, where she knew they would meet the M25 near Thurrock, chuckled when Sue responded with barely concealed bemusement.

"Well, Essex listeners, you've got Callie Hall coming to you live… from the M25. Yes, that M25. Expect traffic updates, drum and bass, and possibly a small existential crisis between junctions. She's also got TOWIE star Jack Gethin with her, and he's got some news to announce."

Callie knew that Jack was a close friend and, even though he was a minor cast member, a The Only Way is Essex alumni, and he was her celebrity endorsement for her campaign. He'd agreed, after some badgering and several pints in a Romford Wetherspoons, to come along for the ride and publicly endorse her campaign. Mostly because he thought it'd be "a laugh", but also because he genuinely liked her manifesto pledge for free WKD Blue for all uni students, alongside Callie's lesser-known policy to "nationalise Chicken Cottage for the vibes."

The Battle Bus creaked as it merged onto the A13, its suspension audibly protesting every bump in the road. The bright-orange paintwork—already half-obscured by layers of graffiti and political slogans—gleamed in the weak February sun. A modest convoy of curious drivers honked and filmed the monstrosity as it pulled ahead. The speakers on the top deck blasted "Don't You Want Me" by The Human League at a volume that surely breached at least three Ofcom guidelines and several laws of physics.

Looking at her phone, which was on the DJ desk, plugged into a USB-C port on the laptop which had Zetta loaded on one screen, WhatsApp on another and on the third had G-Selector, she saw that the generator and arial, which was next to the stairs and above the drivers cab, Richard Hammond being the driver today as he was PSV licenced and so could legally operate the Battle Bus, were both functioning as intended. The audio signal was holding, the Wi-Fi booster tethered to a quintet of 5G routers, mounted on the roof was transmitting the OB feedback to Stratford cleanly, and the Manic Essex studio had already lined up her intro jingle for 4pm.

She glanced at Jordan, who was sat in the Producers chair, who had his own computer and laptop setup with the same software loadout. He gave her the thumbs-up, headphones already half-on, his other hand fiddling with the fader levels on the OB mixer as if he was prepping for a world-ending DJ set rather than a regional radio broadcast about potholes, party politics, and poultry-themed populism.

"You've gone crazy, babes," Jack said with a chuckle. "I mean, I know I got Sugar Pied in Season 22 by someone who said I 'lacked intellectual depth', but this? This is like if TikTok and Newsnight had a baby on a Megabus."

Callie didn't even look up from her notes—if one could call a sheet of A4 covered in neon-pink Sharpie scrawl 'notes'.

"That's the whole point, Jack," she replied, tugging her headset on and adjusting the mic boom. "It's organised chaos. Vibe-led policy. The electorate is bored. I'm giving them something to talk about over their Tesco meal deals and vape shop visits."

Jack nodded slowly, staring out at the endless blur of M25 signage. "And you want me to do the big reveal live on air?"

Callie grinned. "Absolutely. You're not just here as eye candy with dental endorsements. You're our first celebrity backer. You're kicking off the Manic Celebrity Cabinet."

Jack raised an eyebrow. "Mate, I got 18,000 followers and a dog that barks at EastEnders. You sure I count as cabinet material?"

Callie, deadpan: "Jack, I've got a pigeon in sunglasses as our party logo. The bar is low. Anyway, Jordan, nip downstairs babes and get us some WKD, and see if anyone knows how long we'll be til we're on the Dartford Crossing?

Jordan gave her a look of weary amusement, pushed his chair back with a squeak, and carefully descended the narrow staircase that had been installed when the bus was a former TfL bus and, according to one of the Manic Blues hosts who was a bus enthusiast, a former Metroline bus, TAL121 apparently, and therefore had been used on the

113 route out of Edgware back in the early 2000s. Callie had, of course, groaned when it had been relayed in excruciating detail over several pints by a bloke from Manic Blues called Malcolm, had somehow embedded itself in Callie's brain, and now lived rent-free next to the fact that Edgware was in fact a place and not a black hole where souls and trains went to die.

Upstairs, as the engine droned and the Battle Bus bounced over the start of the Queen Elizabeth II Bridge, Callie stared out of the wide panoramic front window. The Thames glimmered to the right, the skyline of Dartford rising in the distance like a strange, suburban mirage. She tapped her foot against the DJ booth casing, drumming out the intro to a track she was mentally lining up—something dramatic, synth-heavy, and deeply inappropriate for peak-time radio.

Even though playout was centrally controlled and so she could only adjust the playout of the local segments on Zetta, not the locked in music.

"Right," she said into her mic, testing the levels as the OB link finalised its handover. She knew that the news would be first, and that was already pre-recorded at Stratford by the newsroom, so she didn't have to worry about cueing it in. But as soon as the bulletins were done, Manic Essex was hers—entirely.

The on-air light flashed on.

And with that, the 4pm news jingle rolled.

She sat back for a moment and let it play out—some grandiose electronic pulse written by the same in-house composer who also moonlighted as a techno producer in Dalston. It made the headlines sound ten times more dramatic than they actually were. Which, given that the lead story was about East Anglia train fraud, someone being fined over £20,000 for a large scale ticket evasion, and an "unidentified stench" on Romford High Street, was saying something.

"And that's your 4 o'clock news across Essex," the smooth, regional voice concluded. "Now, it's time for drive. With Callie Hall… live from the M25."

The Manic jingle thundered in—strobing lasers of synths, thudding bass, and the familiar DJ drop: "Manic Drive— Essex Vibes, with Callie!"

Callie took a breath, threw the fader up, and leaned into the mic.

"Alright, you beautiful lot of road-weary, roundabout-hating legends… I'm coming to you live from Britain's most cursed motorway. That's right. The M25. We're broadcasting from the Manic Battle Bus, somewhere between Dartford and existential despair. I've got a pigeon on my chest, WKD in the cooler, and a former TOWIE reject to my left—Jack Gethin, say hi to Essex!"

Jack leaned into the spare mic and gave it the full Essex charm. "Alright, Essex. Missed ya. I brought the vibes, and… well, they brought the bus. I didn't know what I was signing up for. But here we are."

Callie chuckled, then rolled straight into her opener. "So, I've got tunes, I've got traffic, and I've got political commentary disguised as meme culture. I am your chaos courier for the next four hours. Let's start things off with a banger—here's 'Heads Will Roll', yeah, the A-Trak remix. Because if you're stuck in junction 29 gridlock, you might as well be raving."

She hit the playout.

And they were off.

****

CHAPTER 7 – Breakdown
Friday 23rd February 2024

Of all the things Callie had hoped for on the 117-mile attempt at broadcasting live on Manic Radio Essex Drive from the M25, having to pull over to the hard shoulder at the Heathrow turn-off—Junction 15—was not what she had envisioned.

The Manic Battle Bus, in all its garish, tangerine glory, had been rumbling along fairly smoothly since the Queen Elizabeth II Bridge. Sure, the suspension had growled at every pothole, and yes, the bass from the top-deck DJ booth had been so intense that, being an open topper, it reverberated out of the bottom like a subwoofer in a tin shed, but for the most part, it had held together. Until now.

Callie knew, from Laurence, one of the technical guys at Stratford, that the generator powering the DJ deck and OB kit was separate from the main engine. That meant she could, theoretically, do a six-hour non-stop show without the bus even moving—though, at that point, it would simply be an illegal street party with some light electoral undertones.

But the main engine? That was a reconditioned beast lifted from another Dennis Trident which, according to Malcolm from Manic Blues (who once drunkenly cornered Callie at a Christmas do to monologue about vehicle VIN plates), had been withdrawn from TfL service after an "unfortunate fire in the electrical housing." Naturally, the Battle Bus had inherited its heart from a machine that once caught fire during a school run in Croydon.

"And that was Cardi B with her hit Up," Callie's voice crackled through the OB mic, her tone deceptively upbeat even as the Battle Bus began to stutter beneath them. "Speaking of things going up, the revs on this bus have just done something deeply suspicious. And now... we're pulling onto the hard shoulder, right by Heathrow airport. Anyway, it's half past 6, and I've got half an hour until Manic Prime Evenings with Toni starts at 7pm, so let's all hope I'm not presenting tonight's final link from inside a recovery van, yeah?" Callie added, forcing a chuckle as the Battle Bus gave a shudder and lurched to a reluctant halt beside a ragged strip of grass, tarmac, and tired-looking crash barrier. They had just passed the signage for the M4 interchange, where the traffic from Slough, Maidenhead, and Heathrow all tangled in a slow-motion ballet of bad lane discipline and indicator denial. "I'll be back after the news."

Callie knew that she had to record some links now for London Vibes, as she was 'reporting' live for them from the M25 as well as doing her own show for Manic Essex. She waited for Jordan to load up the link to Studio 1 at Stratford, where Kez and Harper were doing their own drive show from the comfort of the climate-controlled, coffee-scented studios with actual chairs that didn't rattle like a wobbly IKEA skeleton on MDMA.

Meanwhile, the bus beneath her was wheezing like an asthmatic steam engine, and the faint aroma of burnt something—possibly rubber, possibly dreams—was wafting up through the stairwell.

Jordan nodded to hint that the link was set up, and the next thing she knew, she could hear the duo from the sister station was ready to record the link. Harper's voice, cool as ever, came through her monitor, already laced with the deadpan disbelief Callie had grown to adore.

"Alright, as you know folks, we've got our mate from Manic Radio Essex, Callie Hall, live on the Manic Battle Bus, and she's so far endured delays around the M26 interchange, chaos at Clacket Lane, and now, Callie, babes, where are you?"

Callie exhaled sharply, adjusting her headset and hitting the comms button on the OB desk with a dramatic sigh. "Currently? Parked up in the seventh circle of hell, and I don't mean Leicester Square with Lord Ashley and his Pitbull Jenkins over my shoulder. I mean the hard shoulder. Of the M25. Junction 15. Outside Heathrow. Our beloved Manic Battle Bus has finally had enough of my chaotic charisma and decided to take an unscheduled nap."

Harper cackled in her studio. "Wait—you've broken down?"

"Affirmative," Callie replied, eyes fixed on the smoke— or steam, or possibly the lingering spectre of diesel ghosts—drifting from the undercarriage. "We've fully entered the mechanical twilight zone. Hammond's outside kicking tyres, Jordan's inside kicking himself for not getting the AA Premium, and I'm one jam sandwich away from launching a leadership coup against my own party."

Kez's voice joined in, equal parts intrigued and amused. "Tell me you're still broadcasting though. I swear, if this all ends with 'Signal Lost' and you doing the rest of Drive from a Little Chef..."

Callie leaned back in the cracked vinyl chair, flicked a switch on the OB mixer with theatrical flair, and grinned. "I am absolutely still broadcasting. I will be presenting this show if I have to shout it through a traffic cone at the northbound slip road. The vibes are bulletproof. The engine isn't. Anyway, Kez, what's coming up next?"

Callie knew that Kez would say the next track, which, like every other track on the Manic stations at drive, was centralised, so she'd be announcing the same track at 6:34pm, two minutes time, on Manic Radio Essex, the same time as the conversation was being played out on London Vibes, and she knew it was Dario G's Sunchyme. Looking at the clock, she had 18 seconds until the news was finishing, so she'd have to wrap this up fast.

"Sunchyme," Kez replied smoothly, already cueing the line. "Perfect soundtrack for a breakdown. Bit of optimism while you stare into the abyss."

"Love that for me," Callie quipped. "Stuck on the M25, broadcasting from a rave bus that's gone on strike. It's like if 'Trainspotting' had a glitter budget and bad transport links."

She slid the fader up, timing it to the second as the final beats of the 6:30 news jingle faded out. "And that's your regional headlines done, which included a fox attacking a bloke in Chelmsford and—tragically—no further updates on the Romford High Street pong situation. But here's something a little sweeter on the senses. Now, who wants to win a million quid tonight?"

She knew that she had to do the promo spiel for Manic Millionaire, the weekly giveaway where one caller selected on Manic Prime Evenings every Friday at 7pm would win a guaranteed £1,000,000 live on air, no codeword unlike Heart or Capital, no having to remember a money amount like Hits Radio's Cash Register, just a pure and simple cash drop—and she needed to sell it with the same energy she'd use for WKD happy hour.

"Essex, London, Dartford services… wherever you're tuning in from—yes, even you in the Mondeo eyeballing us from the next lane—we've got a million quid with your name on it. It's Manic Millionaire time, babes. All you need to do is pick up the phone if we call you after 7. That's it. No codeword, no fuss, no radio jingle jenga. Just answer like a normal human being and your bank account gets significantly sexier. Jack, how do people enter?"

She saw Jack grab the piece of paper and come over to the mic from where he had been perched on a camping chair near the emergency exit. He cleared his throat with all the dramatic gravitas of someone announcing the lottery numbers on a cruise ship talent show.

"Right, you lot," Jack Gethin said, his thick Essex drawl practically oozing through the OB mic. "If you wanna get your mitts on that million, text MILLION -to 87106 or hop onto our website at manicradioplays.co.uk and click through to enter online. Entries cost £3, but there's also a free entry route, by calling 0330 880 3601, which is included in most phone plans. "

Callie flashed a grin, seamlessly adding, "Its a network competition across the Manic Prime network, so entries are open to anyone listening on any of our stations— whether you're on Manic Radio Essex, London Vibes, Bee Manic, Manic Goldies or if you're a posh git listening to Manic Classical. Lines close at 7 and Toni Green will be calling the lucky winner live at ten past. So keep your phone on, and for the love of all things caffeinated, don't let your nan answer thinking it's a PPI call. You have to be 18 or over, and do get Bill Payer's permission. Anyway, here's Dario G, because tonight is Friday, and know that at 10pm, it's the Manic Dance Takeover with DJ Spanxx here on Manic Radio Essex, so..."

The sound of Sunchyme kicked in as Callie finished talking about the competition, and the mellow, optimistic steel drum intro rolled through the bus speakers, completely at odds with the anxious silence that had taken hold downstairs. One thing Callie noticed was that the timing for the song wasn't the usual radio edit version, but the full 8 minute original mix, which Callie suspected the Liverpool team had ripped from the original record and uploaded to the server, as she could hear the crackles that only came from vinyl. It gave the whole thing a slightly nostalgic, analogue edge that completely clashed with the harsh buzz of diesel anxiety vibrating up through the floor. The 8-minute runtime was a gift though—an oasis in which to regroup, replan, and stretch her legs as the bus was now stationary.

She could see the car behind the bus, the 'Manic Mates', the recently formed street team which followed the Battle Bus in a stickered-up Ford Galaxy filled with street teamers, folding tables, crates of merchandise, and refreshments, all to ensure that the battle bus had sufficient supply for the passengers on board. One of them—Rhiannon, a student from Barking who'd come onboard the campaign after getting suspended from her media degree for submitting a mockumentary about Wetherspoons as her final project—got out of the Galaxy and grabbed a plastic box, which obviously had some form of sustenance and refreshment.

"I'm nipping downstairs for a min," Callie said, knowing she had ten minutes, as Zetta was showing that the next track was Calvin Harris' Ready for the Weekend, and she could let that one run after Dario G while she sorted out her vocal cords with something wet, preferably fizzy, blue, and of dubious nutritional value. She yanked off her headset and descended the rickety stairs two at a time, aware the Battle Bus now echoed with the strangely calm ambiance of late-90s euphoric house. The kind of song that made you want to buy a bucket hat and cry about your A-Levels in a field.

As she reached the lower deck, she noticed that the group of technical people, as well as other Manic staffers who were assigned to the show and also the Battle Bus, from IT to Compliance, were all milling around on phones, while Rhiannon had just boarded and was dishing out Tesco sandwiches and granola bars that had been obtained prior to the departure from Stratford over three hours earlier, and was handing out drinks from a cool bag emblazoned with a spray-painted slogan: "**VOTE VIBES.**"

Hammond, she noticed, was on the phone, obviously calling for a recovery lorry to come and deal with the sudden mechanical collapse of the Battle Bus. His free hand gestured wildly at nothing in particular, like a stressed GCSE drama teacher trying to mime brake failure to a class of hungover sixth formers. His high-vis jacket, thrown on in a fit of duty and dismay, clashed terribly with the fluorescent orange of the bus—like a health and safety Power Ranger who'd lost the will to live.

Callie made her way past the stacked crates of promo gear and half-eaten catering boxes toward the emergency exit, which Hammond had propped open with a bright pink cone borrowed (read: nicked) from a roadworks site near Clacket Lane earlier in the afternoon.

"Any joy?" she asked, cracking open a can of WKD Blue that Rhiannon had sneakily handed her along with a packet of Tangfastics and a Chicken Caesar wrap.

Hammond turned to her, his face a study in every shade of exasperation known to man.

"I've just got off the phone with my old bosses at Diamond. They've got a depot nearby, at Stanwell, and they've agreed to send someone out. Probably within the hour. Might be able to get us towed to a layby or even a depot yard, but if they can't get the parts, we're staying here for the night." He gestured to the offending wheel arch with a theatrical flourish. "Fanbelt's gone. Completely buggered. Probably shook itself loose somewhere between Clacket Lane when we got caught in the chaos, and Cobham, where we had to stop for a pee break, and now its sulking like you when you've been told by the Regional Director that you need to 'tone it down' on Twitter. Which, for the record, you didn't.

Callie grinned, swigging her WKD. "Branding, babes. Can't stop the vibe train once it's left the depot."

Hammond gave a humourless chuckle. "It's not the vibe train I'm worried about, it's the actual bloody engine that's meant to be moving it."

Behind them, the sun had begun to slip behind the edge of the M4 interchange. The glow cast a weird golden filter over the scene—half West London apocalypse, half low-budget Channel 4 documentary about mismanaged youth outreach. Every so often, a plane roared overhead towards Heathrow, and the entire bus rattled like a maraca full of loose bolts.

Downstairs was a hive of quiet chaos. Jordan, headset still slung lopsided over his mop of curly hair, had parked himself by the back door, where the air was vaguely breathable and the signal bars were strongest. He was on his laptop, frantically monitoring playout and the OB feed. Even with a potential recovery operation looming, he was still trying to keep things seamless. The show had to go on—even if they had to broadcast from the hard shoulder.

Jack was sat sideways on a fold-out chair, flicking through Instagram with the casual detachment of a man who had once filmed himself crying on Snapchat because a Wetherspoons had run out of halloumi fries. He looked up as Callie passed.

"Oi, this bloke's just posted a TikTok saying we've caused 'the most chaotic traffic jam since that cow escaped on the M40.'" He held the phone up triumphantly. "Look—we're already viral again. Hashtag 'BattleBusBreakdown' is trending at number 6 in the UK."

Callie took the phone from Jack and scrolled briefly through the trending tag, watching video after video of her bright orange Battle Bus standing wounded at the side of the motorway. Drivers were slowing down to film it, some of them even shouting encouragement out of their windows. One lorry driver had filmed himself honking in rhythm to the Sunchyme beat, and someone had already mashed it together with the video of her yelling "Legal as a late-night kebab and twice as messy" from earlier that week. Another user had posted, "The M25 has officially given up—Callie Hall broke British infrastructure with vibes alone."

She handed the phone back, biting into her wrap. "Right, Jack," she said, mouth half-full, "new plan. We keep rolling content. Even if we're not rolling wheels. You up for a little InstaLive in fifteen?"

Jack nodded, already smoothing his hair with the kind of care only someone who once filmed a skincare haul in a McDonald's bathroom could summon.

She turned back to Jordan. "You good to patch in that next local ID for Essex after Calvin Harris?"

Jordan gave a thumbs-up, then immediately flinched as the Battle Bus made another unsettling *clunk* beneath their feet. The kind of sound that suggested something vital had just fallen off and would shortly be run over by a coachload of confused pensioners heading for Hounslow.

Callie sighed. "Cool. Because after that, we're going rogue. I'm not letting this breakdown be the vibe death of this campaign."

She took one more sip of her WKD, then made her way to the small desk at the back of the lower deck where a bunch of spare OB kit had been stacked in case of emergencies. To her delight, someone—probably Laurence—had packed an old battery-powered Rode mic setup and a mini tripod. That meant InstaLive was very much back on the table.

"Okay, people," she called, voice echoing across the bus. "Show of hands: who's staying on the Battle Bus for a shoulder broadcast spectacular and who's defecting to the Manic Mates car like traitors to the cause?"

Tash, the ever-beleaguered events producer, groaned from her seat near the kitchenette. "I'm only defecting if the Galaxy has biscuits."

"No," Rhiannon shot back, poking her head up. "All we've got is three mini cans of Pepsi Max and a broken folding chair. Vibes only."

"Then we're all staying," Callie declared. "And this—" she gestured around her with mock grandeur, "—this becomes the scene of our triumph. Tonight, the Manic Battle Bus doesn't die. It *rebirths* itself. Like a chaotic phoenix. From the ashes of broken fanbelts and shattered expectations."

Hammond grunted from his seat at the front. "You're giving Churchill at Dunkirk, but for a rave bus."

Callie grinned. "Exactly."

It was nearly 10pm, three hours after the Manic Radio Essex Drive show had ended, and Callie, Jordan and the Battle Bus crew were sitting in the Diamond Bus South East depot at Stanwell, as they were waiting for a Diamond driver to come on shift to run a Private Hire service to take them to Stratford, while the bus was on a low loader, heading to Stratford itself, where it would be parked in a covered building which was its home in London when not being used, due to it being open top and not a closed roofed vehicle. The team were sat under humming strip lights, surrounded by the heavy scent of diesel, chip-fat-scented uniforms, and the comforting background buzz of vending machines that hadn't been restocked since the early stages of the Johnson government.

"Right, it seems our bus back to Stratford is one of the Hotel Hoppa buses," Hammond said, with all the enthusiasm of someone who had been condemned. "And no, it's not one of the newer ones, but one of the older ones."

Callie, now wrapped in a faded tartan travel blanket that had been mysteriously pulled from one of the Manic Mates' crates—either a relic from a Christmas OB in Dundee or a promotional leftover from Manic Goldies' "Warm Hearts Winter Tour"—gave Hammond a look of mock horror over the rim of her WKD Blue can.

"Oh brilliant," she drawled. "We've gone from neon-drenched election chaos to getting chauffeured home in a branded airport bus that shuttles tourists to their hotel and does endless loops of Heathrow."

"Yep, it's one of those. Funnily enough, I did my PSV test down here when it was National Express who ran the Hoppa, and they had these buses called B6s. Volvo abominations that got replaced by the things that we're about to board. And before you ask—yes, they still smell like disappointment and Lynx Africa."

Callie gave a theatrical groan, pulling her travel blanket tighter and slumping sideways onto Jordan's shoulder. "I swear, if we end up sharing with a stag do from Luton looking for Terminal 3, I am going to resign from my own party and declare myself a nation-state."

Jordan, now nursing a barely warm flat white from the depot's vending machine, muttered, "You already act like one."

The depot door creaked open, revealing a man in a weathered navy uniform, his name badge reading "Norman" in faded block capitals. He blinked at the assembled chaos huddled around the vending machines and battered sofa set like a half-drunk focus group for Trainspotting: Radio Edition.

"You lot the ones going Stratford?" he asked, his accent somewhere between Slough and pure, unfiltered exhaustion.

Hammond nodded. "That's us. Cheers for taking the late shift."

Norman shrugged. "Don't thank me yet, mate. This thing rattles like an old Zippo lighter and the heater's on the blink. But it's got wheels, and it moves, so up you get."

The team groaned en masse, grabbing bags, promo crates, and leftover wraps. Jack tried to smuggle a second can of WKD into his hoodie, only to have Rhiannon snatch it from him with a pointed "one per person, Tory."

Outside, the bus idled like an ageing dog. Callie noticed that it was a 2008 vehicle, looking at the reg plate, so was at least sixteen years old and still being flogged around west London like a pensioner with a gym membership they couldn't cancel. The livery on the side was advertising autenticacuba.com, a tourism website promoting Cuban holidays, though the wrap was peeling off near the back door and the flag had sun-faded to the point it resembled a poorly printed Pride logo. The interior was dimly lit and smelled faintly of reheated rice, pine cleaner, and air-con that hadn't been serviced since the London Olympics.

Callie hoisted herself up the step with a sigh. The seats were those faux-leather things that made your thighs stick if you sat down too fast, and every time the bus jolted into gear, a worrying rattle echoed from beneath the floor.

"Well," she muttered as she slumped into a seat near the middle, "at least it's a ride. Beats calling an UberXL with 13 crates of pigeon-themed merch."

***

CHAPTER 8 – Crash Course
Wednesday 28th February 2024

The fluorescent lights buzzed overhead in the hastily-booked community centre conference room, a brutalist leftover from 1970s Newham municipal planning. The walls were a faded magnolia, the carpet a grey-blue swirl of wear and tea stains. Fold-out chairs were arranged in two uneven rows facing a battered whiteboard on wheels. A flipchart leaned drunkenly in the corner, one of its pages already defaced by someone's crude drawing of a pigeon in sunglasses—Callie's campaign mascot had made its mark.

Callie Hall stared at the room like it was a GCSE exam she hadn't studied for. "This place smells like weak tea and broken dreams," she muttered, nudging Jordan with her elbow.

"Bit like your campaign then," he shot back with a grin, before instantly regretting it.

Callie narrowed her eyes. "Excuse me, my campaign smells like rebellion and cherry WKD. Get it right."

"Morning!" boomed a voice from behind the whiteboard, startling everyone. From behind it emerged a man in his late fifties, tall and willowy, with a shock of unruly grey hair that looked like it had been styled by sticking his head out of a high-speed train. He wore a long corduroy coat over a faded graphic tee that read "MAKE MEDIA STRANGE AGAIN."

Dr Simon Ellerby, media consultant, eccentric academic, and alleged former advisor to three politicians and one minor royal, swept into the centre of the room like a conductor about to direct a very chaotic orchestra.

"Dr Simon Ellerby," he said, dramatically adjusting invisible spectacles that he wasn't wearing. "Media strategist, behavioural theorist, caffeine addict. And you"—he pointed dramatically at Callie—"are late."

Callie held up a Costa coffee that she had, in a rush obtained from the Costa at Stratford rail station, as her Overground train from Romford had ran late, and sighed. "Sorry, mate, I had to get a flat white before I got here. Can't campaign on an empty bloodstream, can you?"

Dr Ellerby gave an indulgent smile, the kind a weary teacher might give a particularly sarcastic teenager. "Caffeine is essential, yes, but punctuality is power. Remember that. Now—welcome, all of you, to the Crash Course. Capital C. Capital C. In political media warfare. Now, all of you are from Independent and small party candidates planning to appear in the 2024 Local and Mayoral Elections, yes?"

Callie raised her hand as though she were in a Year Nine Citizenship class. "What if you're from a party that's not small in spirit, but like... metaphysically chaotic?"

Dr Ellerby blinked at her, then broke into a grin. "Ah. You must be the DJ Pigeon Candidate."

"That's me," Callie said proudly, thumping her chest. "Callie Hall. Drive presenter, youth ambassador for chaos, and humble emissary of the Manic Collective. We believe in vibes, free WKD, and banning Capital FM."

A polite ripple of confused laughter ran through the room. Some of the other attendees—an independent candidate from Redbridge in a suit three sizes too big, a Lib Dem councillor with a tired face and even wearier hair, and a Green Party hopeful in a fleece adorned with hand-drawn badges—turned to look at her with equal parts bemusement and fear.

Jordan, sitting behind Callie with his Manic Radio-branded notepad, sank slightly in his seat.

Dr Ellerby clapped his hands. "Wonderful. It's always best to begin with disruption. Democracy itself is built on it. Now then! This morning session is titled 'Messaging in the Mayhem: Crafting Narratives in the Content Apocalypse.' Subtitled—" he dramatically flipped the whiteboard to reveal a scrawled diagram that looked more like a conspiracy theory map than a media strategy, "—'Don't Be Boring.'"

Callie nodded sagely. "Finally, someone who gets it."

Daisy Round, perched on the edge of her fold-out chair with a suspicious sausage roll from the community centre vending machine, leaned over to whisper to Jordan, "Is this bloke for real?"

"Depends what dimension you're asking in," Jordan replied, scribbling 'Narrative = Chaos + Authenticity?' onto his pad like it might one day make sense.

"Let's begin with *authenticity*," Dr Ellerby intoned, pacing in front of the whiteboard like a TED Talk speaker on a tight budget. "What is it? Who has it? Who fakes it? And why do voters lap it up like it's the last pint of Strongbow in a dry pub?"

Callie raised her hand again.

"Yes, the Chaos Emissary?"

"Is it when you're too poor or too defiant to hire a PR consultant so you just sort of tweet whatever comes into your head?"

"Bingo," said Dr Ellerby, spinning dramatically to write "*AUTHENTICITY = UNFILTERED TRUTH + STRATEGIC SPONTANEITY*" in marker pen that immediately began to squeak and dry out.

"But don't get it twisted!" he declared. "Unfiltered doesn't mean unhinged—well, not always. Strategic spontaneity is the art of appearing unrehearsed while secretly planning everything. It's chaos... choreographed."

Callie looked offended. "You mean my chaos is *staged*?"

"No," said Ellerby, wagging the marker. "Yours is just particularly compelling chaos. But we're going to *refine* it."

Callie folded her arms. "I don't want to be refined. I want to be left the hell alone to cause political whiplash and make people laugh at how ridiculous it all is."

"Then congratulations," came a new voice from the back. "Because that's exactly why you've gone viral."

All heads turned as a young woman in a bright pink hoodie emblazoned with the words *"I POST THEREFORE I AM"* strutted into the room with an iced matcha in one hand and a TikTok ring light in the other. Her phone was already clipped in and recording.

"Hannah Pritchard," she introduced, without pausing. "TikTok consultant, viral manipulator, and part-time nihilist. I've been brought in to make sure none of you old farts flop online."

"Except me," Callie said, grinning. "I'm already a digital menace."

Hannah Pritchard raised one neatly threaded brow. "Exactly why I asked to shadow this session. You've got natural 'main character syndrome,' but now we're going to weaponize it."

"Wait," muttered the Lib Dem councillor, adjusting his lanyard nervously. "Is this still part of the official training?"

"It is now," Dr Ellerby said brightly, gesturing like a magician revealing a trapdoor beneath a top hat. "Politics isn't just knocking on doors and shaking hands anymore. It's memes, livestreams, viral moments. You need to be ready for the platform war. Think Question Time meets Love Island meets WWF SmackDown."

"WWF?" the Redbridge Independent candidate asked, slightly confused.

"Back when it was still cool," Callie supplied. "Before pandas ruined everything."

Dr Ellerby gave her a wink, as if she'd just earned a bonus point in some invisible game. "Now then," he said, striding back to the whiteboard and sketching a wobbly triangle. "Let's talk about the Content Trinity: Platform, Persona, Punchline."

He scribbled furiously, marker squeaking like a rodent in distress.

"Platform: where you show up. Persona: how you show up. Punchline: what people remember. Your campaign needs to exist at the intersection of all three."

Callie leaned forward, tapping her pen against her notepad. "So, like… DJ Pigeon posting about free WKD on Instagram while I'm stuck in traffic on the M25 counts as a punchline?"

"Correct," Hannah said, plopping her ring light onto a nearby desk and angling her phone towards the class. "Because it wasn't just funny—it was sticky. Shareable. Absurd. But with intent."

Daisy raised her hand. "What if your content's not chaotic, just like... very sincere? Are we doomed?"

"Not doomed," Hannah said with a shrug. "But you better be compelling. Or really hot. Preferably both. Otherwise, TikTok will eat you alive."

The Green Party hopeful looked vaguely traumatised.

"Don't worry," Ellerby said, sensing the unease. "This isn't about being fake. It's about controlling your narrative. Politics is theatre. You can either act, direct, or get written out in the first scene."

Callie let out a low whistle. "Someone's been listening to Manic Goldies late at night."

Ellerby bowed slightly, acknowledging the reference. "Only during the jazz reruns."

Hannah clicked her nails against her iced matcha. "Let's do a little test. Everyone: what's your one-line pitch? Like, elevator pitch but for the internet. If someone had to describe your campaign in ten words or less, what would it be?"

Muttered silence.

The Redbridge Independent said, "Empowering communities through shared responsibility and increased local funding."

Callie stifled a yawn.

The Lib Dem councillor said, "Fiscally responsible investment in sustainability for a fairer London."

Hannah's face was blank. "Sorry, I fell asleep halfway through that."

Callie raised her hand. "Mine's 'Vibes, value meals, and pigeons in positions of power.'"

Ellerby gave her an approving nod. "Now that is content."

Jordan scribbled it down automatically. "I'm putting that on a T-shirt."

"Already being printed," Hannah said, glancing at her phone. "Your fanbase has started a Redbubble page. One design has you in a crown made of WKD bottles. Someone else did a pencil sketch of DJ Pigeon in front of Parliament like it's 'Les Mis'."

Callie beamed. "I love democracy."

Dr Ellerby tapped the whiteboard, sending a ripple of anticipatory silence through the room. The squeak of the dry-erase marker had become oddly comforting, a sonic anchor in this storm of eccentricity and electoral intrigue.

"Right then," he continued. "Since we've established that messaging, authenticity, and chaos need to coexist harmoniously, let's move on to your interview strategies."

Callie immediately groaned, slumping dramatically lower in her seat. "Oh God, here we go."

Ellerby gave a wry smile. "Now, Callie, as our resident provocateur, you need special training. You're charismatic, chaotic, memorable—but currently, you're also reckless. Reckless can be good, but controlled reckless is better. Think of this as media aikido: using their attack as your momentum."

Callie sighed, glancing sideways at Jordan, whose expression was a mix of bemusement and genuine curiosity. He shrugged, mouthing the words "aikido?" at her. She mimed throwing someone to the floor. He raised his eyebrows appreciatively.

"First rule of interviews," Ellerby announced grandly, uncapping the marker with dramatic flair, "answer the question you wish you'd been asked."

The Lib Dem councillor blinked. "You mean…don't answer the actual question?"

"Precisely," Ellerby grinned. "Well, not unless it's helpful to you. This is called pivoting, and it's an art form. Observe."

He pointed the pen at Callie. "Callie Hall, why is your campaign so frivolous?"

Callie flicked her hair over one shoulder, sat up straighter and plastered on a mock-serious expression. "Great question, Simon. But the real issue we should be addressing is why the other candidates are so painfully dull. I mean, if you're not laughing, are you really engaging with democracy? The Manic Collective isn't frivolous—it's disruptive, imaginative, and more importantly, it's getting young people to care. Plus, we give out free WKD. Which is more than you get from a leaflet promising 'sensible stewardship of fiscal frameworks.'"

The room laughed, albeit nervously. Even the Green candidate cracked a smile.

"Excellent!" Ellerby clapped. "That's exactly the energy. Now, imagine doing that live on LBC, but without getting flustered or accidentally calling the host a knobhead."

Callie narrowed her eyes. "That happened once. And to be fair, he *was* being a knobhead."

"Nonetheless," Ellerby said diplomatically, "media aikido. Redirect, reframe, reassert."

"Sounds like my dating strategy," Callie muttered.

"Moving on," Hannah jumped in, already angling her phone to catch Callie's expression in three-quarters profile. "We're going to do some TikTok pitch drills now. Ten seconds. To camera. Tell the internet why they should vote for you."

Callie perked up, twisting in her chair to look directly into Hannah's ring-lit phone. "Right now?"

"No time like the algorithm," Hannah said.

Callie took a breath, smoothed her hair, and grinned. "I'm Callie Hall, Drive presenter turned vibe minister, and I'm here to paint Westminster neon orange. If you want politics with playlists, pigeons and perfectly chaotic energy—vote Manic. Vote vibes."

Hannah nodded approvingly. "That's already got 200 views, and we haven't even posted it properly. You've got that chaotic-girl-who-knows-what-she's-doing energy. Gen Z eat that up like pastel stationery."

"Do *you* want pastel stationery?" Callie asked, already mentally adding it to the merch list.

"Later," Hannah said, focused on clipping the sound into a trend-ready format. "Now someone else try."

The Redbridge Independent candidate nervously stood. "I'm Nigel. I'm running as an Independent because I believe in… in transparency and… and… erm… fiscal integrity—"

Hannah winced. "Okay, no. Stop. That's a GCSE oral exam, not a TikTok. Smile. Say something punchy. Use your eyebrows."

"My eyebrows?"

"Look, either move them or don't, but they've got to mean something."

Callie leaned back, watching the carnage unfold with great enjoyment. Daisy kicked off her shoes, swinging her feet beneath the chair and whispering to Jordan, "It's like watching an episode of The Apprentice, but with more badge lanyards."

"I feel like I've aged four years in this room," Jordan replied, eyes on his pad, where he was currently sketching DJ Pigeon mid-glide, holding a sign that read *NO MORE LEAFLETS. JUST LASERS.*

Ellerby let the workshop continue until the clock struck noon and a bell rang from somewhere in the depths of the community centre, possibly to signal the arrival of the dreaded *tea trolley*. A tall man in a branded hoodie that read "Gerry's Civic Catering" wheeled in a plastic cart laden with industrial-strength tea, instant coffee, custard creams and suspicious-looking egg mayo triangles. The smell of overboiled water and powdered milk swept the room like a storm.

Callie perked up. "Oh, good. Democracy fuel."

Daisy inspected the teacups with the cautious precision of a museum archivist. "This one still has lipstick marks. And not mine."

"It's all part of the flavour," Callie said, dunking a custard cream into a steaming cup of tea that was more beige than brown.

Ellerby reconvened them ten minutes later. "Afternoon session! We're talking field strategy. Hustings. Hustle. Ground game."

"Which is why I'm going round the Unis with the Manic Battle Bus from tomorrow with lots of WKD," Callie said with a grin, still chewing on the custard cream like it was fuel for rebellion. "That and going to the different town centres... oh, and a day in Leicester Square, with mini pigeons and QR codes."

"And we're parking the bus right outside Capital's HQ with 'Ban Capital' all over it," Jordan then added to Callie's sentence, grinning as she leaned back on her plastic chair, arms behind her head like she'd just solved a particularly challenging Sudoku puzzle.

The room audibly gasped. Not in the scandalous, tabloid-horror kind of way—but in the "she's actually going to do it" kind of way. The Lib Dem councillor dropped his custard cream. Even Dr Ellerby paused mid-sip of the world's weakest coffee, his eyes gleaming with something between admiration and foreboding.

"You're... planning a publicity stunt outside Capital Radio's headquarters?" he asked cautiously.

Callie nodded. "Full OB rig. DJ decks. Banner that says 'Silence the Static. Ban Capital.' DJ Pigeon in a foam suit. Probably some kind of legally grey confetti cannon. And Jack Gethin in a feather boa reading out listener complaints."

"You realise," Ellerby said slowly, "that Capital FM is owned by Global. As in, multi-billion-pound media empire with very large lawyers and even larger libel departments?"

"Good," Callie said, slapping her hands onto her knees. "They'll hear us coming. Anyway, it's backed by Manic Radio, Global's biggest competitor, so it's not as if Manic can't cover it under 'content creation and strategic provocation'. Besides," she added, smirking, "I'm not naming individuals. I'm criticising systems. And I'm doing it with a pigeon mascot and a fog machine. If anything, that's performance art."

As the group shifted uneasily in their fold-out chairs, Dr. Ellerby seemed to reconsider his initial reaction, his eyebrows knitting together with curiosity. "Performance art?" he repeated, tapping the edge of his plastic mug with a contemplative look. "I suppose it could be seen that way. Provocative, yes. Effective? Well, that's a whole other matter."

Callie gave a lazy grin, unconcerned by the wariness in the room. "That's what this campaign is all about, Simon—pushing boundaries, making people think, making them laugh. And yeah, if it all blows up in our faces, at least we went out with style. It'll be the most talked-about thing in media for a week. Maybe more."

Jordan, who had taken to doodling DJ Pigeon in various absurd political poses on his notepad, looked up at her with an approving smirk. "She's not wrong," he added. "Callie's been trending non-stop since we kicked off. That Capital FM stunt? If it happens, it'll break the internet. It's already viral in the making."

The room seemed to breathe a little easier after Jordan's endorsement. The Lib Dem councillor, who had been clenching his fists around a custard cream like a man facing the firing squad, glanced over at Callie with something akin to genuine respect. "I'll admit... it's a bold strategy. But it might just work."

"Thank you!" Callie exclaimed, raising her mug of tepid tea in a salute. "It's bold, it's in-your-face, and it might be completely ludicrous, but that's exactly why it'll grab attention. Who said politics had to be dull?"

"Unfortunately, most of the electorate," the Green Party hopeful muttered under his breath, clearly not fully convinced.

Callie, ever the diplomat when it came to her own chaotic brilliance, winked at him. "Well, it's your job to try and make it less dull. I'm just here to disrupt."

Hannah, who had been obsessively editing her phone's footage of Callie's pitch, chimed in, her voice practically vibrating with excitement. "Honestly, this is the kind of content that can change everything. Politics is shifting, right? It's more about the *moment* now than about the *message*. People are tired of hearing the same old promises. They want real, raw moments that feel like they could have been taken out of a meme. And that's where you shine, Callie."

A slight pause hung in the air before Dr. Ellerby cleared his throat, the weight of his words about to drop like a hammer. "Alright, alright, I'm starting to see the logic here," he said, rubbing his temples. "But what happens when the fun stops and the serious stuff comes into play? Vibes can't run a city, can they?"

Callie leaned forward, her hands clasped in front of her. "You'd be surprised, Simon. The fun? It doesn't stop. Not when you've got a platform that engages an entire generation of voters who've never even considered voting before. When they hear 'ban Capital,' they hear 'we're sick of the same tired political party lines that never change anything.' They hear someone finally calling it out for what it is. And that's powerful."

"Exactly," Jordan added, scribbling something in his notebook. "It's not just about the memes or the slogans. It's about sparking conversation. Giving people a voice through the noise."

The room was starting to warm to the idea, though not all were fully sold. The Lib Dem councillor still looked uncomfortable, possibly wrestling with the idea that his own carefully crafted campaign platform—built on polished talking points about sustainability and fiscal integrity—might pale in comparison to the chaotic whirlwind of Callie's approach.

Dr. Ellerby, ever the intellectual, nodded slowly, his mind clearly turning over the idea. "So, we're talking about creating noise that cuts through. But noise doesn't always lead to lasting impact. That's where the content strategy will need to evolve." He glanced over at Callie. "If you want to be the disruptor, you need more than just shock value. You need to frame the narrative. That's where the punchline matters."

Callie cocked an eyebrow. "You want me to stop making jokes, Simon? That's where I shine."

"No, no, not stop," he said, waving his hands in the air as if trying to catch a fleeting thought. "But let's take it a step further. Look at the election debates, for example. Who's going to remember the speeches on transport? On housing? They'll remember the candidate who makes them laugh, but also the candidate who can speak to real issues in a way that feels fresh."

Callie took a deep breath, taking in what Ellerby was saying. "So, what you're telling me is, I have to keep pushing the chaos while still focusing on the real stuff?"

Dr. Ellerby gave a satisfied nod. "Exactly. The question is—can you make the chaos meaningful?"

****

CHAPTER 9 - Flyposting
Wednesday 6th March 2024

The can of spray glue hissed in Callie's hand like a snake with attitude. In the other, she gripped a rolled A2 poster like a baton, ready to baton-charge democracy. Under the dull flicker of a cracked sodium lamp beneath a railway bridge just off Hackney Wick, she flattened the poster with the practised grace of someone who had once wallpapered an entire student union toilet with anti-Brexit memes.

DJ Pigeon—glaring from behind his oversized headphones and surrounded by chaotic slogans in blocky neon font—was now officially staring down traffic at 2am on a Wednesday. The caption? ***"VOTE VIBES. BAN BOREDOM."***

Callie knew that technically what she was doing was illegal, but she didn't care, as she was going for that vital demographic of disenchanted 18-to-30-year-olds who hadn't voted in the last two general elections, but *had* once gone viral for throwing shapes in a Lidl car park at 3am. This wasn't about appealing to the electoral commission's idea of order. This was about making a mess—one that stuck.

Behind her, Jordan McCabe was fumbling with a rucksack filled with more of the same posters, plus a roll of neon orange gaffer tape, a pouch of biodegradable cable ties, and three hastily stolen traffic cones for "aesthetic disruption." He adjusted the Manic Radio lanyard that still hung from his neck, not because it helped tonight, but because it reminded him that this was sanctioned chaos—sort of.

"I swear, the next time you say 'just one more street,' Callie, I'm going to make you glue your own trainers to the pavement," Jordan muttered, crouching beside an abandoned Santander Cycle dock, currently serving as their makeshift base of operations.

Callie ignored him, already stepping back to admire the freshly adhered poster.

Daisy Round emerged from around the corner, her hoodie pulled low, and a high-vis vest slung over one shoulder. "That's poster number thirty-two," she whispered, nodding toward the bridge arch as if confirming a kill count. "And Shaun's just gone rogue again—he's tagging the hoarding outside the Olympic Aquatics Centre with the slogan '*PIGEONS NOT POLITICIANS*' in bubble graffiti."

"Legend," Callie muttered, reaching for another poster roll.

Shaun "Sticky" Willis—graffiti icon, muralist, and professional municipal headache—had been roped into this particular bout of electoral vandalism after Callie met him at a community arts event where he was painting a socially conscious Banksy parody on the side of a pop-up vegan sausage van. Callie had introduced herself by handing him a WKD and saying, "Do you want to start a political movement with a bird in shades?" Somehow, it had worked.

Now, armed with a hoodie reading "Austerity is Theft" and an antique stepladder he'd nicked from his mum's garage in Romford, Shaun was halfway through transforming the Queen Elizabeth Park's outer wall into a swirling, phosphorescent mural featuring DJ Pigeon breakdancing on the heads of faceless politicians.

Back in Hackney, a faint sound of distant sirens cut through the calm.

Jordan looked up, his face etched with concern. "That's the second one we've heard since Tower Hamlets. You reckon someone's called us in?"

Callie waved her hand dismissively. "Mate, this is Hackney. Sirens are like seagulls in Brighton. Doesn't mean they're for us."

But she still worked faster.

Daisy held up a folded copy of their schedule—hand-scrawled on the back of a Manic Radio Essex cue sheet. "Next stop's Shoreditch High Street. We've got eight minutes until Sticky meets us at the Costa by the overground station."

"We're doing the station frontage?" Jordan asked, eyes wide.

"Yup," Callie confirmed. "All of it. DJ Pigeon's getting prime commuter eyeball real estate. Nothing says 'legitimacy' like being next to a Pret A Manger and a bloke on a Lime bike with a podcast."

They moved in bursts. Camden Lock. Clerkenwell Road. Outside a gated development in Elephant and Castle where the residents definitely didn't want a revolution, let alone one led by a pigeon. With each stop, the posters multiplied—each one a jolt of political defiance in lurid orange and yellow, scrawled with phrases like:

"POWER TO THE PECKING CLASS"

"MAYORS SHOULD RAVE, NOT WAFFLE"

"FIX TFL OR I'LL DJ AT LEICESTER SQUARE AGAIN"

Sticky kept pace, vanishing and reappearing like a spray-paint spectre, always two moves ahead, always with one eye on the skyline for choppers. He barely spoke, except to occasionally grunt "Move," or "Nice drop," or to mutter "I should've been a dentist" whenever a tag smeared mid-line.

** _ * _ * _ **

By 3:45am, London was beginning to tremble awake. Bin lorries groaned their metallic yawns through Tower Hamlets. Uber drivers queued idly at red lights, oblivious to the battle of billboards taking place around them. A few foxes darted across the roads like suburban ghosts. And everywhere Callie and her crew had been, DJ Pigeon looked on—vibrant, smug, defiant.

The Manic Collective had successfully claimed twenty-three intersections, eight Tube station hoardings, four construction scaffolds, and at least one bus stop roof.

"Alright," Callie exhaled, standing under the purple glow of the Shoreditch High Street sign, her fringe stuck to her forehead with a heady mix of hairspray and condensation. "We've covered the East."

Jordan, wheezing like he'd just completed an off-brand Tough Mudder, dropped his bag with a thud. "We've also technically committed five misdemeanours and an act of extreme visual terrorism against the O2 mobile shop façade."

Daisy, calmly sipping from a flask of lemon squash she had inexplicably kept in her coat pocket all night, shrugged. "Eh. You know it's a good campaign when you end up on CCTV more than the actual mayor."

Sticky arrived last, hoisting himself up the steps from the side of the bridge, his eyes red but focused, his hoodie now splattered with teal and orange from a particularly ambitious wall in Bethnal Green. He tossed a final spray can into a nearby bin with the precision of a disillusioned Banksy and nodded. "Done."

Callie grinned, stretching her arms like a conquering general surveying a battlefield strewn with undercaffeinated yuppies and empty vape pods. "And not a single clipboard in sight."

"Y'know," Sticky said with a grin. "We could always nip over Seven Sisters tomorrow, to the tube depot there, and tag a few trains, or look on TfL's website, find the Working Timetables, find which tubes park up in the stations and sidings and not the depot, and get them with DJ Pigeon."

Callie lit up at the idea like someone had handed her the electoral equivalent of a golden ticket. "You're saying… we turn DJ Pigeon into rolling stock propaganda?"

Sticky nodded solemnly, as though he'd just proposed a cross between the Suffragette movement and the opening sequence of Trainspotting. "Picture it: a Bakerloo line train, 5:45am service, rolls into Elephant and Castle, and what's that on the cab door? DJ Pigeon. Right next to the No Entry sticker. Bloke in a suit looks up from his overpriced flat white and boom—he's voting vibes."

Daisy snorted into her flask. "It's political messaging via public transit infrastructure. I love it."

Jordan, however, looked less convinced. "You do realise that spray painting a live Tube train is not just illegal, but like… properly illegal? As in, anti-terrorism-level illegal."

"And?" Sticky said with a grin. "I'm already known to TfL as a tagger, and I've got like lots of community service under my belt from back in the Boris era. They'll just fine me and make me paint over something in Croydon again."

Callie put a hand to her mouth, partly to stifle a yawn, partly to suppress a very real laugh. "I mean, Sticky, that's either the dumbest thing I've heard all campaign—or the best. Paint a vibe, pay a fine, repeat. It's practically performance tax. Fuck it. go on, we'll do it," Callie said, blinking slowly through the streetlamp haze like someone having a divine revelation outside a kebab van. "We tag the trains. And not just DJ Pigeon—we do issue slogans.

We co-opt the commute. We weaponize platform five at Walthamstow Central."

Jordan groaned, dragging a hand down his face. "Callie, we're not Banksy. You don't just pop out of bed with a stencil and a dream and not get arrested on CCTV ten minutes later."

Sticky scratched his chin, which was lightly peppered with paint flecks. "Go girl, we'll do it. Anyway, we can do both spray and clings. Magnetic vinyl. Stickers. High-grade shit that stays on through half a rush hour before a TFL cleaner clocks it."

"Magnetic vinyl?" Callie repeated, half in disbelief, half in glee. "You're telling me we can slap DJ Pigeon on a Northern line train and have it vanish like a magician's calling card before TfL even gets the kettle on? I'll get Manic's print unit to do some clings and shit. We've got nearly £175,000 left in the budget, so if we can blow five grand on glow-in-the-dark lanyards for the Manic Mates, we can definitely afford magnetic vinyl of DJ Pigeon flipping the peace sign on a Jubilee line train."

Jordan groaned, but even he couldn't suppress the grin that followed. "Fine. But if I get arrested, I want it to be for something more dignified than holding a step ladder for a pigeon."

Callie snorted. "Please. Nothing is more dignified than this. This is the civil disobedience of our generation."

"Yeah, Jord, stop being a bore," Daisy said with a grin, slapping Jordan lightly on the back with the rolled-up copy of the cue sheet. "This is graffiti with purpose.

Stickers with soul. If Banksy can flog a shredder painting for a million, we can stick a pigeon on the Bakerloo and call it radical infrastructure commentary."

Jordan pulled a face, the kind only a tired, morally conflicted radio producer can manage at nearly 4am. "Just so we're clear: your version of 'field campaigning' involves flyposting, industrial-strength glue, sticker bombs, and possibly breaking into a train depot?"

Callie didn't even blink. "Yep."

He threw his hands up. "Fine. But I'm not wearing a balaclava. Last time I wore one, I got mistaken for a Deliveroo rider and forced to carry a bag of frozen katsu past Barking."

Daisy leaned back against the Shoreditch station railings, unbothered. "You wore a balaclava to Barking? That's on you, mate."

"Focus!" Callie said, suddenly clapping her hands like a drama teacher trying to rally Year 10s before a dress rehearsal of *An Inspector Calls*. "We've still got the university drops, the chicken shop outreach, and we've got to finalise the Stratford rave OB."

Jordan groaned. "Not the Stratford rave…"

"*Yes*, the Stratford rave," she replied, eyes gleaming with mischief. "You think I'm going to let DJ Pigeon fizzle out with a whimper? No way. We're going to project the party manifesto in twenty-foot text onto the Westfield glass at midnight, like it's Gotham and we're summoning a discount Batman."

"Is the manifesto even finished yet?" Daisy asked.

"Almost," Callie said, fishing a folded sheet of paper from her back pocket. "Here's what we've got so far—tell me it doesn't slap."

1. *Free WKD Blue for students on polling day.*

2. *Ban Capital FM for crimes against taste.*

3. *Introduce a Night Mayor who actually DJs.*

4. *Nationalise Chicken Cottage.*

5. *Convert Zone 1 Pret A Mangers into rent-controlled housing.*

6. *Legalise post-10pm raves in municipal car parks.*

7. *DJ Pigeon becomes the official London mascot.*

"Is number seven legally binding?" Jordan asked.

"Only if we win," Callie said, with a wink.

"I can't tell if this is politics or an elaborate game of Cards Against Humanity," he muttered.

"Anyway, we need to hurry up, as I've got a cover shift in an hour on London Vibes," Callie then said with a yawn, as she looked at the time and noticed how it was 4:47am. Callie blinked against the grainy light bleeding into the sky above Hackney, her face lit by the amber streetlamp glow and the blue-white screen of her phone. The adrenaline that had fuelled the night's chaos was beginning to flicker and fade, leaving behind only exhaustion, glitter, and a mild sense of giddy delusion.

"I've got to be in Stratford in half hour for prep," she muttered, rubbing her eyes with the back of her hand, narrowly missing a smear of dried poster glue on her sleeve. "I'm covering the early show on London Vibes. Luke and Gazza are off, so I was asked yesterday to cover their slot, 6am till 10. Apparently I'm the only one mad enough to do a full graveyard campaign shift and still sound semi-coherent on live radio."

"Barely," Jordan said, shaking his head. "You sound like someone doing a TED Talk inside a Wetherspoons kitchen."

Callie gave him the finger and drained the last of her now lukewarm Costa flat white. "And yet, somehow, I'm still more electable than half the ballot. Right, let's wrap this."

Sticky was already folding his ladder with practised grace, like a street magician who knew when the curtain needed to fall. Daisy collected the empty spray cans, stuffing them into a bin liner that definitely wasn't labelled for recycling but would do in a pinch. Jordan wrestled the now-crumpled master cue sheet into something approximating a folder and slung it into his bag.

"Stratford in thirty," Callie muttered, her voice low, half to herself, half to the city. "DJ Pigeon's watching. And so is the algorithm."

The group melted into the pre-dawn quiet of Hackney, the hiss of early buses and the squawk of real pigeons slowly returning to the streets they had so colourfully defaced. Every lamppost they passed bore the mark of their campaign. A slogan. A sticker. A pigeon in oversized sunglasses telling the city to "Vote Vibes."

They weren't politicians. Not really. Not yet.

But they were here.

And they were bloody loud.

* _ * _ * _ *

"Morning London, it's 6:02am, you're listening to Callie Hall, live on London Vibes, bringing you the biggest tracks from the 90s to today, waking up your commute. Gazza and Lukey boy are off today, so I'm filling in with tunes, tea, and a sprinkle of trouble—because nothing says 'rise and shine' like a mayoral candidate with residual glue under her fingernails and the faint smell of WKD in her hair. Anyway, today, I want to know what you've got planned for this weekend, and if you'll come join me at Jubilee Gardens this Saturday, as I've got WKD Blue for over 18s, and nomination forms, as I need at least 330 signatures to officially stand for Mayor of London. That's ten from every borough, babes. So, if you've ever voted, nearly voted, or just moaned about the price of the Overground, I want to hear from you."

Callie leaned back in the London Vibes studio chair, sipping a fresh coffee a runner delivered as Zetta played the first track of the day, Dua Lipa's Training Season, a recently released single by the London based artist, and chuckled as she saw that Tariq al-Murad, the London Vibes breakfast producer, was groaning at her and her microphone antics from behind the glass, mouthing *stick to the link sheet"* while waving a clipboard in mild despair.

Callie gave him a cheeky wink and tapped the side of her headphones like she was taking a direct transmission from DJ Pigeon himself. Then, leaning back into the mic with the kind of swagger that only came from sleep deprivation and righteous conviction, she said:

"Let's be real, London. What do you want in a mayor? Boring promises about bus timetables and vague gestures at climate targets? Or someone who'll turn city hall into an actual vibe zone with policies that slap, slogans that bang, and DJs on the roof terrace every Friday lunchtime? I'm not here to polish boots. I'm here to chuck glitter into the engine room of democracy. So, send in your voice notes—tell me why you're mad at the city, and I'll tell you how we're going to mess it up until it's better."

A text flashed across the studio screen.

Darren in Canning Town: *"She's insane but she's got a point. I've been stuck on a council waiting list since the Olympics. At this point, I'd rather take my chances with DJ Pigeon than any of the last three mayors."*

Callie cackled into her mic.

"There it is. We've reached peak policy fatigue, babes. When the pigeon feels like a more trustworthy public servant than someone in a navy suit with a 'housing plan' written by Deloitte. Anyway, Darren—thanks for your text, and I'll see you at Jubilee Gardens. You bring your signature, I'll bring the WKD."

Tariq slumped forward dramatically in the producer's chair like a man who had just accepted that chaos was now not only inevitable but scheduled on the quarter hour.

The next voice note came in from Chloe in Wood Green:

"Morning Callie, just wanted to say, I love the campaign so far. Me and my flatmate saw one of the posters on our way back from the pub and she's been saying 'Power to the Pecking Class' non-stop for three days. Also, how do I get one of those glow-in-the-dark DJ Pigeon lanyards?"

Callie lit up. "Chloe, babe, we've got crates of them. Come down Saturday and we'll kit you out like you're headlining Glasto's civic engagement stage. And tell your flatmate she's an honorary Pigeon Sister. DJ P's watching."

She flicked a switch on the Zetta playout and Dua Lipa segued neatly into the next song—*"Midnight City"* by M83. A little on-the-nose? Maybe. But the city *was* waking up, and the night's rebellious residue was still clinging to her hoodie, her breath, her brain.

"Coming up," she said, "we've got the headlines at half past. Yes, I'll read them, no, I won't editorialise them too hard. And then we're talking about political branding. If your campaign was a band, what genre would it be? Because mine is somewhere between early grime, Britpop, and absolute chaos core."

The texts kept flowing.

Marvin in Walthamstow: *"Honestly just vibing with this show. Haven't voted in years but if I see that pigeon on a ballot paper, I'm ticking it."*

Laura in Lewisham: *"Wait is that the same Callie who DJ'd my cousin's wedding and crowd surfed into the bar? ICON."*

Georgie in Mile End: *"Tell Sticky the mural near Roman Road SLAPS. Absolute legend. Also, do you have stickers I can slap on my Deliveroo bag?"*

Callie laughed again. "We're a campaign of the people, for the people, by the people who occasionally break minor municipal by-laws. Yes to the stickers, Georgie. Deliveroo democracy starts now."

She sat forward, dropped her voice into something smooth and vaguely sultry—like a midnight DJ voice trying to seduce Ofcom into submission.

"Right, London, this Saturday, Jubilee Gardens. DJ Pigeon meets the public. From midday to six, we're vibing, raving, and collecting those all-important nomination signatures. If you're 18+, bring ID, bring a pen, bring your weird political grievances. We've got a booth where you can record your moan about London, and we'll mash it into a remix. There's free WKD, obviously. Merch drops. And a live OB from the Manic Battle Bus if we can get it out of the depot in time. If not—look for the big inflatable pigeon. That'll be me."

****

CHAPTER 10 – Jubilee Gardens
Saturday 9th June 2024

Callie Hall awoke in Studio 4 of the Olympic Park Studios in a tangle of sleeping bag nylon, glittery socks, and a dangerously lukewarm can of Rubicon Mango, the morning light already streaming through the cracked top window of the Battle Bus. She'd passed out sometime around 3:20am, midway through editing a remix of angry commuter voice notes layered over a breakbeat instrumental of "London Calling". At some point, Jordan had draped a throw over her legs. She assumed it was Jordan. Could've been Daisy. Could've been Sticky. Could have been Linus, as she was covering the Manic Dance Takeover, a Friday night 10pm to 2am show on a pop-up station called Manic Pride, a LGBTQ+ friendly brand which was aimed mainly at the TikTok-fuelled Gen Z crowd who thought acid house was a new brand of vape. Either way, she was stiff, under-caffeinated, and the unmistakable hum of a pre-event panic hung in the air like Febreze over a teenager's gym bag.

She sat up slowly, her hair resembling the back end of a hedgehog, and blinked as her vision adjusted. The studio, one of Manic's 30 Olympic Park studios used for podcasts, conventional and DAB/pop-up stations, and also experimental livestreams that no one had quite figured out how to monetise yet, was in a state somewhere between chaos and charisma. Posters were peeling slightly from the windows. A half-eaten multipack of Space Raiders balanced precariously on the mixing desk. A DJ Pigeon plushie had been zip-tied to the mic boom arm at some point during the night and now stared down at Callie like a hungover conscience in wraparound shades.

She groaned and rolled her shoulders, brushing crumbs off her hoodie and reaching for her phone. 6:52am. Jubilee Gardens Day.

The Big One.

She knew that Manic's Head of Legal and the Lite Group Director responsible for ensuring that she didn't accidentally trigger an injunction, a by-election, or an MI5 file, had obtained a copy of the electors register, so she knew if the person was a valid voter. But the rule was, she needed ten from each borough. Not just ten vibesy uni mates from Tower Hamlets who'd show up for free WKD and dance to her remix of "Get Lucky" with Sadiq Khan soundbites layered over the top. No. Real, human, local electorate signatures, distributed with spreadsheet-level precision.

The fact that she already had 50, some from different universities who she had spent the previous day going round, and a MP who had been convinced she was a Reform candidate and that she was merely conducting "an innovative outreach programme for the disillusioned youth," helped. But she still needed hundreds more. And not just warm bodies with permanent marker scrawls on questionable clipboards. These had to be clean, legible, borough-correct signatures. Because when the Electoral Commission came calling, they wouldn't accept "Greebo69 from Insta" as a valid nomination from Brent.

Callie shoved her phone in her pocket and stood, her spine audibly cracking like a DJ cue point. Outside the studio, the glassy pavements of Stratford were glistening with that annoyingly springlike drizzle that somehow managed to be both refreshing and miserable. She pulled the DJ Pigeon hoodie tighter around herself and blinked against the light.

Smelling her armpits, she noticed that she reeked of a uniquely potent blend of anti-static spray, Red Bull Zero, and stale glitter. Not ideal for a prospective mayor, but perfect for the chaos candidate of 2024. With no time for a shower and no desire to subject Stratford Westfield's facilities to her current state, she did what any self-respecting rave-punk politician would do—she emptied half a bottle of Impulse into her hoodie and called it a compromise.

*_*_*_*

The Battle Bus was already rumbling with life by the time Callie reached it. Hammond had arrived at the crack of dawn, as promised, in a puff of sour vape smoke and resigned muttering about "ungrateful Gen Z revolutionaries" and "bloody pigeons with branding strategies." The engine grunted into action with the sort of mechanical sigh that suggested it wasn't just the humans who were sleep-deprived.

Inside, Jordan was hunched over the sound desk on the upper deck, fiddling with levels and trying to make the flatbed subwoofer stop popping every time someone said the word "vibes" into a mic. Daisy was lying flat on the bar counter with a cold pack pressed to her forehead, groaning theatrically every time a notification pinged on her phone.

"Where's Tash, Sticky, Hammond, and the Manic Mates?" Callie asked, hoping that her voice scratchy with sleep and studio air.

Jordan didn't look up from the desk. "Tash is already on-site sorting the banners and the vinyl tablecloths. Sticky's over at the London Eye tagging the Eye with pigeons, Hammond's gone for a piss, and the Mates? Half are setting up in Jubilee Gardens, half are getting dressed in pigeon outfits, and then there's Rhiannon who is at the Offie getting the bulk order of WKD Blue and Stella... oh, and Duncan has kidnapped Ian Beale... yes, he's kidnapped the actual Ian Beale. Oh, and your TOWIE mate who's the official celeb endorser is meeting us at the Gardens. He's bringing the whole cast."

Callie blinked, trying to process the news. "Ian Beale? Why on earth would Duncan kidnap him?" she muttered, shaking her head in disbelief.

Jordan sighed without looking up. "Don't ask. Duncan's got a... well, let's say 'special' relationship with soap stars. Apparently, he's convinced Adam Woodyatt is some sort of EastEnders oracle who can spiritually bless the campaign by appearing in a TikTok with DJ Pigeon and a smoke machine."

Callie stared, wordless for a beat. Then: "That's... weirdly on-brand. I love it."

Jordan muttered something about this isn't what they taught me at Westminster Uni and went back to fiddling with his levels. The Battle Bus gave a wheeze as Hammond returned, muttering something about the Stratford McDonald's having run out of napkins and "this country being finished". He climbed into the driver's seat and turned with a grimace.

"You've got an hour until public access opens," he warned. "We're doing a test crawl to Jubilee Gardens, then you're flying solo till I collect you after dark. I've got a Moonlight Minicabs shift in between, so don't crash the bastard thing."

"We don't drive it," Callie said, still groggy. "It's stationary political theatre."

"Good," Hammond grunted. "Because last time you tried to reverse it out the depot, you nearly took out the Stratford cycle superhighway."

Callie gave him a thumbs-up with a grin and vanished upstairs, ducking beneath the half-slung bunting that someone—probably Tash—had strung between the poles of the DJ booth. The top deck had been transformed overnight: inflatable pigeons in varying sizes had been tethered along the perimeter railings, all in a matching shade of 'Manic Orange'. A cardboard cut-out of Callie herself, complete with a spray-painted mayoral sash and a slogan reading ***SHE'S BANTASTIC*** in bubble graffiti, leaned beside the mixer table. DJ Pigeon plushies were zip-tied to the ceiling like fuzzy sentinels.

"Right," Callie muttered. "Let's make democracy weird again."

*_*_*_*

It was 12pm, lunchtime, and Callie knew that Jubilee Gardens would be packed to the rafters, not just with London natives, but also tourists from across Europe and the UK, as it was near the London Eye, a major tourist hub. And today, it had been transformed into the unlikely epicentre of Britain's most anarchic political movement.

The Battle Bus had arrived like an alien mothership, juddering to a halt beside the entrance to the green with all the grace of a mildly hungover gorilla. DJ Pigeon's face loomed from its flanks, sprayed large and proud next to slogans like "*NO MORE BORING RADIO*" and "*VOTE VIBES*". As the side panel hissed open to reveal the neon-lit DJ booth and bar-style seating above, Callie emerged from the top deck like a miscast messiah, sunglasses on, WKD can in hand, and a smile that screamed, "Let chaos commence."

The Manic Mates—her street team of Gen Z interns, out-of-work promo reps, and one very confused sociology lecturer on sabbatical—had set up the outreach tent with impressive efficiency. The vinyl tablecloths were already pinned down over the folding tables, the clipboards stacked neatly beside stacks of leaflets that promised a "New Deal for London" and a "Free Packet of Space Raiders With Every Signature".

By the time Callie made it to the foot of the bus, Daisy was already handing out lanyards to curious passers-by, while Tash barked orders into a walkie-talkie as if she were directing a rave-themed emergency services drill.

"Where's Sticky?" Callie asked, adjusting her hoodie.

"Still tagging. He's working on a thirty-foot mural of DJ Pigeon DJing the House of Commons collapse. Said it'll be ready by five," Daisy said, thrusting a clipboard into her hands. "Right, we've got the electoral registers to check names against the nominations, we've got the Data Protection documents that Robert insisted we have to give to anyone who signed on the dotted line, and we've got a load of pens that Kyler nicked from the stationary cupboard."

Callie groaned, as Kyler Thompson, who had brought his 4 year old son, Link, on board the Battle Bus that morning dressed in full junior pigeon regalia—complete with fluffy tail feathers stitched onto a Primark puffa—came swaggering over with a grin so wide it practically deserved its own postcode. Kyler, the walking red flag to women, a man who had more partners, some more willing than a club night guestlist, was wearing a Manic Collective bomber jacket that had been customised with the words *"FLOCK LEADER"* spray-painted across the back in Day-Glo green.

"Callie, babes," he called out, slapping her on the shoulder with the kind of energy that could fuel a mid-range EDM festival, "the turnout is *mad*. I've seen three YouTubers, two people who think they're on Taskmaster, and I swear down, someone's just set up a vape tasting table next to the chicken nugget petition booth."

Callie blinked. "What chicken nugget petition booth?"

"Oh," Kyler grinned, clearly proud. "Link made one. He reckons McDonald's should bring back the old recipe for BBQ sauce, and he's already got 47 signatures. I think one of them's Diane Abbott, but it might just be someone with the same glasses."

"What's that prick doing here?" a voice came from behind the inflatable DJ booth—gravelly, unimpressed, and coated in ten layers of morning-after sarcasm. It was Shanice Turner, East London Hits drivetime host and veteran Manic voice of reason, stepping into Jubilee Gardens with the expression of someone who'd seen too many tech failures and not enough HR compliance.

Shanice stood in full battle mode—aviator shades, a long faux-fur coat (despite it being unseasonably mild), and boots that had clearly stomped their way through a hundred pub-based OBs. She glared at Kyler as if he was a Wetherspoons breakfast menu come to life.

"Did I not explicitly tell you," she said, stalking towards him, "to stop bringing your child to semi-legal campaign events where there are open flames, industrial glue and at least two taggers on the run?"

Kyler held up his hands, the picture of performative innocence. "Hey, Link's part of the movement! He's the youth wing!"

"Did Toni give her consent," Shanice said, her hands on her hips, "to you doing this, or did you assume that because she's a coke addict and is too busy reviving her OnlyFans from a cabin in Llandudno, that full parenting rights had reverted to 'the chaos collective'?"

Kyler winced. "Okay, that's a bit—"

"No, mate," Shanice cut him off, jabbing a finger into his chest, "this is a political campaign. Not a family therapy roadshow with sequins and WKD. You lot have turned the South Bank into a bad acid flashback from 2004. That's why… I've decided to vote for Count Binface."

Callie, to her credit, didn't flinch. She took the clipboard Daisy had given her, stepped past Kyler and Shanice, and clambered onto the makeshift crate-stage in front of the Manic Battle Bus. A wind caught her hoodie as she did, lifting the pigeon-emblazoned hem like a windsock as she adjusted the mic taped to the top of an upcycled tripod stand.

The gathered crowd, a blur of phones, vape clouds, glitter, and suspiciously ironic slogan T-shirts, shifted as the mic squealed into life. Someone in the back shouted "FREE THE PIGEON!" and someone else who might've been on mushrooms responded, "The pigeon is already inside all of us."

Callie raised her can of WKD like a chalice.

"London!" she shouted. "Are you tired of beige candidates with beige policies serving up beige nonsense from beige buildings with beige slogans? Are you tired of parties who care more about votes than vibes? Who promise a better commute and then give you rail strikes and a bus that smells like wet dog and broken dreams?"

The crowd responded with a cheer—some half-ironic, most half-cut. A Manic intern launched a confetti cannon, which immediately exploded far too early and covered

Callie in gold foil. She batted it off her face and kept going.

"I am not here with a manifesto written by think tanks or hedge funds. I'm here with a manifesto co-authored by chicken shop queues, night bus passengers, and people who've ever tried to rent a flat in Zone 3 and been offered a cupboard under the stairs for two grand a month!"

More cheers. A chant began somewhere to the left of the Battle Bus: *DJ Pigeon! DJ Pigeon!*

"And I," she bellowed, "am not running for Mayor of London just to smile nicely on BBC Politics Live while Susanna Reid asks me about my housing policy. I am running because someone has to say what we're all thinking."

She paused for effect, letting the tension rise. Then:

"Bollocks to beige."

The crowd erupted.

* _ * _ * _ *

"Sheesh," Callie said, five hours later when they had got back to the Olympic Park studios. "That was knackering and exhilarating in equal measure."

Her voice was hoarse, the kind of dry rasp that clung to the back of the throat like overplayed promo jingles on regional CHR stations. She collapsed into a mismatched beanbag in Studio 4, legs akimbo, the lanyard still dangling around her neck like a prize from a particularly unruly tombola. The Manic Battle Bus had returned to the depot with a screech of its rusted brakes, Hammond already threatening to "defect to Smooth FM if they keep defiling my bus," while Sticky had vanished somewhere near Bromley-by-Bow with a backpack full of vinyl clings and the manic grin of a man on a mission.

Across the room, Jordan was sprawled over a battered studio chaise longue, the sort of thing no one admitted to ordering but that had inexplicably survived three rebrands and a scandal involving an ill-fated intern rave in 2019. Daisy sat cross-legged at the mixing desk, editing voice notes into an audio collage for Monday's campaign podcast, fingers flying across the touchpad like she was DJing a jazz funeral for democracy.

"Final tally?" Callie croaked, already anticipating the worst.

Jordan groaned, half-turning to check the spreadsheet on his phone. "Three hundred and thirty-seven."

Callie sat up like a spring-loaded scarecrow. "You're shitting me."

"Nope," Jordan replied, eyes bleary. "Ten per borough. Plus a few extras from rogue borough floaters who just liked the vibe."

"And they're all legit?" Daisy added, not looking up from the screen.

"As far as the registers go. Robert from Legal's already cross-checking handwriting samples like he's doing GCSE forensics. Told me two of the Camden ones had suspiciously identical 'g's."

Callie gave a breathy laugh of disbelief, rubbing her eyes with the sleeve of her hoodie. "Mate… we did it."

"You did it," Daisy corrected. "We just provided the legal buffer, glitter cannons, and a frankly disturbing number of ClipArt pigeon stickers."

Callie was silent for a moment, staring at the ceiling, at the flickering LED strip that pulsed with fading neon. Then she sat forward and grabbed her phone.

"Right. If we've got the numbers, that means Monday's the registration. We're going to City Hall."

"Are you...sure?" Jordan asked. "I mean, it's one thing to have a giant inflatable pigeon and a manifesto that includes nationalising Chicken Cottage, but it's another to walk into a government building and officially declare war on the political establishment."

Callie locked eyes with him, all the mad clarity of someone who'd mainlined WKD and public sentiment for seventy-two hours straight. "We've already declared war. This is just the legal paperwork."

****

CHAPTER 11 – Livestreaming the Deposit
Wednesday 20th March 2024

It was the day after the notice of election had been published by City Hall, and Callie knew that she was going to have to do something big. Not just another outside broadcast with clipboards, nor another street rave that got picked up by LadBible and misquoted by The Telegraph as "a sponsored rave by George Soros".

No… this was the day they would livestream the payment of her £10,000 deposit.

The moment she clicked open the notification from Robert-from-Legal, confirming the formal deadline for mayoral candidates to lodge their nomination forms and the deposit, her eyes widened. She had a week and a half until she had to lodge the nomination forms and the deposit, and she knew that most candidates would either turn up quietly with a staffer and a banker's draft, or use a solicitor. But Callie Hall? The Chaos Candidate? She was going to turn it into a full-blown media event. A livestream. A political performance. A vibes-powered protest against boring politics. And, if she could pull it off, a viral masterpiece.

Callie Hall was sitting cross-legged in a battered, squeaky office chair that had probably witnessed more marketing brainstorms and hungover podcast edits than any furniture should be subjected to. Studio 4 buzzed with fluorescent urgency—cables tangling across the floor like they were trying to unionise, Daisy shouting something about frame rates, and Jordan repeatedly muttering "I swear to God, if one more person touches the HDMI splitter..."

The Battle Bus was parked outside like a sleeping dragon—still daubed with neon slogans and half a packet of Cheesy Wotsits melting on the dash. DJ Pigeon, zip-tied to the upper deck's railings, had developed a slight lean from the wind, giving him the posture of a disco evangelist deep in prayer.

"Okay," Callie said, swigging a rapidly warming can of Diet Irn-Bru. "Here's the vision: we don't just pay the deposit. We livestream the payment from the steps of City Hall with a full-on procession."

Jordan, still editing last night's TikTok from their "Manifesto Karaoke" stunt in Hoxton, didn't even look up. "A procession."

"Yeah. Like a wedding. Or a weird pagan ritual. We bring the £10k in a transparent Perspex cube. On a trolley. Carried by... pigeons."

Daisy blinked. "Human pigeons?"

"Obviously. No actual birds. RSPB would end us."

She wheeled her chair round dramatically, knocking over a crate of campaign stickers, and jabbed a finger in the air like a revolutionary dictator fuelled by WKD and passive-aggressive feminism.

"We don't just submit. We announce it. We say to every sad-faced beige-suit policy muncher in City Hall: we're here, we're loud, and we have legal tender."

"Not if it's coins," Jordan muttered. "There's a limit on how much you can legally pay in coins. The Banking Act. Robert said."

Callie ignored him. "We're doing it in fivers. Glitter-coated fivers."

Daisy groaned. "The Bank of England will kill us."

"Then it'll be martyrdom by banking. The ultimate Gen Z political tragedy."

Callie looked up to see David Cole, the Head of PR for Manic's Olympic Park hub, and Tash Crozier, one of the Events Producers walk in, and she knew that they'd be the ones who would either greenlight this madness or send her back to the drawing board with a health and safety risk assessment and a strong word about defamation clauses.

David, a wiry man who looked like he'd once been a stressed-out press officer for a touring grime festival and never quite recovered, folded his arms. "Right," he said, voice heavy with the kind of corporate weariness only built through years of influencer damage control. "What's this I hear about pigeons and money laundering?"

Callie grinned. "It's not laundering if the glitter's biodegradable."

Tash, dressed in a hi-vis jacket despite being nowhere near a construction site, just shook her head. "You want to drag a Perspex cube full of fivers through the streets of London to City Hall?"

"No, not drag," Callie corrected. "Parade. There'll be a parade. Marching band, maybe. I've got Sticky working on a papier-mâché DJ Pigeon float. The deposit is just the climax."

David exhaled so slowly it sounded like a dying fax machine. "Do you understand how tight a rope we're walking here between anarchic genius and being sectioned under the Mental Health Act?"

"Mate," Callie said, standing with the gusto of someone who thought caffeine could replace sleep, "if we do this right, it's not just news—it's culture. This will be the most viewed nomination livestream in British electoral history. That's legacy stuff."

Tash gave a slow, considering nod. "Alright. But only if we get clearance from Robert. And Sticky doesn't set fire to anything."

Callie pumped her fist. "Yes! Operation Cash Parade is a go."

* _ * _ * _ *

The marching band, much to Callie's dismay, had been banned, as the Head of Legal, Robert, had determined it might "constitute unauthorised street performance in a controlled civic zone." So too had the papier-mâché float—Sticky's ambitious two-metre-tall sculpture of DJ Pigeon decked out like the Pope riding a glitter cannon. Tash had seen the prototype and declared it "emotionally disruptive and physically unstable."

Instead, Operation Cash Parade was scaled back to what was now known, half-mockingly, as Deposit Walk: The Livestream.

The plan was simple: a small but visually potent procession from Tower Bridge to City Hall. No more than eight people, all in coordinated outfits—orange boiler suits with holographic pigeon feathers stitched to the backs. Callie insisted on wearing a cape. Jordan had begged her not to.

"Please," he whispered, as she posed in front of the cracked studio mirror. "Please, no capes. You're not a Marvel hero, you're barely even a functioning adult."

Callie fastened the Velcro with theatrical precision. "That's where you're wrong. I'm not a Marvel hero. I'm an origin story."

Looking at Kyler, who had decided to skip the Manic Radio South Coast Breakfast, leaving Lucy Bell, his co-host since 2023, when the third part of the trio, Sarah Wilkes, had quit after Kyler had tried to sexually assault her, to which she reported to Manic's management who had decided to sweep it under the carpet and threaten her with a lawsuit if she spoke out about the incident, the irony wasn't lost on Callie. Kyler, once again unpunished and thriving, had now fashioned himself as the self-declared "Pigeon Chancellor" for the day. His boiler suit was zipped open halfway to reveal a mesh vest covered in glitter, and the words "I RUN ON VIBES AND POOR IMPULSE CONTROL" sharpied across his chest.

"You know, it's going to be funny how we're bringing a pigeon bank filled with £10 grand in pound coins to City Hall to pay for your inclusion on the ballot," Kyler said, his grin so wide it practically needed planning permission. "It's like an avian-themed Robin Hood moment. But make it ravecore."

Callie looked at the Perspex pigeon shaped piggy bank, which contained exactly 10,000 £1 coins with tiny LED lights wrapped around each bundle like it was Christmas at the Bank of England. She exhaled through her nose, one part exhilaration, one part mortal dread.

"It's legal tender," she muttered. "And besides, it's not money laundering if it glitters."

"Still sounds like a strong start to a BBC Panorama episode," Jordan replied, balancing the livestream rig on his shoulder with the cautious air of someone who had already lived through two near-fatal TikTok collapses and an open flame incident involving Sticky, a vape, and a dodgy glitter cannon.

"I ran the numbers," Daisy called from across the room, where she was trying to sync the livestream with five platforms simultaneously. "We've got full YouTube coverage, Insta Live, TikTok Live, Facebook and Kick."

Kick, Callie knew, was an Australian platform known mainly for chaotic gaming streams and the occasional unfiltered political rant. Fitting, then.

"…and Twitch banned us," Daisy added brightly, adjusting her monitor. "Apparently the account got flagged for 'excessive poultry-themed content' after the DJ Pigeon Hour last Friday."

Callie winced. "It was a rave set with feather boas. How is that obscene?"

"Someone reported it as 'avian-coded fetish content'," Jordan deadpanned. "And, honestly, given Sticky's outfit that night, I don't blame them."

They all turned momentarily as Sticky burst in through the fire exit, arms filled with boxes of high-vis sashes emblazoned with VOTE VIBES OR DIE in pixelated comic sans.

"Just got these back from the printers!" he grinned, dropping them onto the nearest table in an explosion of fluorescent thread and questionable kerning. "Also, I found a bloke down in Dalston who reckons he can 3D print a rotating DJ Pigeon helmet for the City Hall handover moment."

Daisy shook her head, not even looking up. "If we give the Electoral Commission staff PTSD, we are not getting on the ballot."

* _ * _ * _ *

As the Manic Collective arrived at City Hall, Callie noticed one person who was, according to most of the Manic drivetime hosts, herself included, the bane of Manic's drive slot, as they, much like Capital and Hits Radio's drive shows, had, in some areas, a show which was in the Top 4 most listened to shows.

Tony Lee.

The Drive host for the all national, all DAB, radio station Smash Mix.

A station formed of former Bauer and Manic bosses, Smash Mix was a glossy, over-produced Frankenstein's monster of CHR tropes, AI-assisted music scheduling, and fake TikTok audio designed to go viral while never really saying anything. Its playlist was fifty per cent algorithm, forty per cent focus-grouped nostalgia bangers, and ten per cent Tony Lee smirking like he'd invented youth culture.

There he was, standing on the steps outside City Hall in an offensively tight blue blazer with a microphone branded with Smash Mix's garish lightning-bolt logo, flanked by a junior producer wearing Beats headphones like a badge of honour and filming everything on a gimbal that looked more expensive than most community radio OB rigs.

But Tony wasn't looking happy.

In fact, he was looking like he was going through the motions, as if someone had kicked his puppy and he had to smile through it for the cameras. Callie grinned, sipping from a neon pink water bottle full of caffeine and indignation. She recognised that expression. That was the look of someone who'd been scooped. Who'd thought he was going to be the headline act on this particular patch of democratic theatre, only to find out the rave circus had beaten him to the stage with glowsticks and a bird mascot.

"Morning, Tony!" she called out cheerfully, ascending the steps with a flair that could only be described as 'pantomime messiah.' The cape billowed. The coins jangled ominously inside the Perspex pigeon piggy bank on wheels behind her, pushed by two of the Manic Mates dressed in head-to-toe holographic lycra with novelty beaks strapped to their faces.

Tony looked up. His eyes narrowed. "Oh, wonderful. It's you. Just what I needed on this shitter of a day."

Callie grinned as she reached the top step, bouncing slightly on her heels as the bustle of camera flashes and phone lenses closed in around her.

"Aw, c'mon, Tony," she chirped, spreading her arms wide as if the whole democratic infrastructure of London were her stage. "Cheer up. It's a great day for democracy. And pigeons. Mostly pigeons."

Behind her, the Perspex pigeon piggy bank rattled forward with a dignity it absolutely did not deserve. The coins inside glittered under the weak March sunlight, as if money itself had decided to go clubbing. Sticky, now acting as the ceremonial "Pigeon Treasurer," dabbed at his forehead with a napkin he'd filched from Greggs, his sash slightly askew and his LED shades flickering like a broken fairground ride.

Tony sighed audibly. "Well, when you've been told your employer's going under and the only thing standing between you and redundancy is a 'Meme of the Month' competition judged by an AI that thinks Riz Ahmed is a weather pattern... you stop seeing the funny side."

Callie froze mid-pose. "Wait… Smash Mix is—?"

Tony nodded with the weary sadness of a man who'd once played Calvin Harris on seven consecutive drive shows. "The bank that's backing us pulled the funding. Some City type who sees a £20,000 loss as a personal insult and decides to pull the plug on a ten-million-pound media venture. We had our last 'core audience retention call' this morning. Bloody Mason, Potter and Associates. Their overlords at Lloyds have decided to throw us into administration. You know, it's that bad, with Global, Bauer and Manic cutting shows to the bare bones, I've had to put a bloody application into the BBC."

Callie's manic grin faltered.

Not out of sympathy—she had about as much empathy for Smash Mix as a pigeon did for a Tesla—but out of morbid curiosity. The radio apocalypse was accelerating, and here stood one of its shiny casualties in an off-the-peg Zara blazer, clutching a Smash Mix mic like it was an expired Oyster card.

As it was the only CHR station in the UK that was commercial and not local, Callie knew that Smash Mix had only national networked programming, with national only ads, whereas the other three stations—Manic, Capital and Hits—still retained some vestiges of local opt-outs or remnants of regional identity, even if only for OFCOM compliance and news bulletins. But Smash Mix had gone all in on the dystopia—one brand, one voice, one blindingly artificial drive host calling every listener "legend."

And now it was dying.

Callie's mind whirred as she stepped past Tony, her grin sliding back into place like it had been cued by an offscreen producer. She turned, raised her arms theatrically once more, and declared, "Let it be known that on this day, the people's candidate deposited not just coins, but chaos, colour, and commitment to a London free of beige radio."

One of the Manic Mates let off a party popper. A sad little poof of paper confetti flopped onto the stone steps and was immediately carried off by the breeze, like the last shreds of Smash Mix's target demo.

Tony gave her a half-hearted middle finger before turning back to his cameraman. "Let's go live, Adam. And make it moody. Channel four o'clock news energy."

* _ * _ * _ *

Inside the ground floor of City Hall, the atmosphere was one of studied politeness being gradually poisoned by performance art. The security guard at the front desk blinked in disbelief as the Perspex pigeon was wheeled towards him, followed by a trail of beak-clad interns and a woman in a cape humming "London Calling" under her breath.

Callie approached with the wide, sincere smile of someone who knew they were either making history or earning a life ban from government property.

"Hello! I'm here to formally submit my nomination to stand as Mayor of London under the banner of The Manic

Collective." She gestured with both hands to the pigeon. "And this is the deposit. All £10,000 of it. In shiny, sequinned, totally-legal pound coins."

The security guard stared at the money-filled bird for a long beat, then picked up the phone and muttered something unintelligible to whoever was on the other end. Callie caught the words "transparent poultry" and "is this even legal" before he hung up with a grimace and nodded her through.

"Right, you'll want Electoral Services, which is down the corridor, past the vending machines, left at the portrait of Boris Johnson, and into Meeting Room B. Someone from the nominations team will meet you there. But for the love of God, don't block the fire exits with that thing."

Callie turned to her crew, who had begun inching the Perspex pigeon forward like it was a prized float in a low-budget carnival. "You heard the man—mind the fire exits. Also, be cool. This is the serious bit. And by serious, I mean: please don't shout 'bollocks to beige' until we're officially confirmed."

Sticky gave a solemn nod, one LED lens flickering mournfully.

The group followed the instructions of the security guard to get to Meeting Room B, City Hall's least charming offering, a windowless box of bureaucratic neutrality, its walls were painted the colour of a PowerPoint background, and the carpet tiles bore the unmistakable aesthetic of "bulk order from an unfortunate tender".

Meeting Room B did not want to be famous.

It was not designed for chaos, or even moderate interest. It was the room you stuck last-minute procurement interviews in, the room where somebody's PR intern cried into a Lidl egg salad sandwich after learning they'd accidentally sent an embargoed press release six hours early.

But today, its soul-destroying beige carpet, its stackable grey chairs, and its flickering halogen lights bore witness to something new: The Arrival of The Chaos Candidate.

The pigeon entered first.

Wheeled by Rhiannon and Duncan, who wore mirrored aviators and full-body glitter catsuits, it squeaked slightly on the door frame, caught on the lip of an uneven tile, and then surged forth with the momentum of a bargain bin supermarket trolley containing ten thousand pound coins.

Callie followed in full regalia: cape trailing behind her, neon eyeliner like war paint, and a manic grin that suggested she'd either slept three minutes or thirty-five hours. Nobody was sure which.

A confused electoral officer named Claire looked up from her desk, nearly knocking over her municipal mug emblazoned with "WORLD'S OKAYEST DEMOCRACY ADMINISTRATOR." She blinked. Once. Twice. Then did what any sensible civil servant would do in such a moment: she reached for the stapler, as if arming herself.

Callie beamed. "Claire! Hi! I'm Callie Hall, submitting my official nomination for the London mayoral race. This is my legal deposit. It's in coins. But also vibes."

Claire stood slowly. "Right. Um. You've brought... ten thousand pounds. In pound coins. In a bird."

"It's a pigeon," Rhiannon corrected helpfully. "With civic integrity."

Claire nodded slowly, a bureaucratic reflex. "You're aware this isn't a bank, yes?"

Callie grinned. "It's City Hall. It's where democracy lives. Which means it can take the occasional novelty bird full of financial symbolism."

Claire pinched the bridge of her nose. "Okay. You've got the nomination forms?"

Daisy stepped forward, passing a neatly collated folder across the table. "Signed. Sealed. Spreadsheeted. Ten signatures from every London borough. Verified against the electoral roll. Robert-from-Legal nearly burst a blood vessel doing handwriting checks."

Claire took the folder, flicked it open, and started thumbing through the pages. The silence that followed was broken only by the gentle hum of the vending machine outside the corridor attempting to murder a can of Sprite.

"I have questions," Claire said eventually. "Many. Some about this form. Some about your mascot. And quite a few about how one even transports ten thousand pounds in coins across London without violating anti-terror protocols."

"We used the Jubilee Line," Duncan offered. "Off-peak."

Callie leaned forward. "Claire. If I may. This isn't just a deposit. It's a statement. It's about visibility. About disrupting the beige parade of modern politics. This is about reclaiming public space—not just physical, but political."

Claire looked at her for a long moment. Then nodded. "Fine. I've worked here thirteen years. You're only the third candidate I've had submit in fancy dress. But definitely the first to bring a pigeon bank. Sit down, and we'll go through the forms together."

****

CHAPTER 12 - Stratford Stand-Off
Monday 8th April 2024

The Manic Battle Bus looked utterly unrepentant in the morning drizzle, defiant in its obnoxious neon glory as it sat straddling the eastern edge of the Olympic Park car park. The sky was a leaden grey, pigeons swirled overhead like something out of a GCSE art project gone moody, and yet the scene was anything but solemn. The bus itself, covered in a kaleidoscope of neon spray paint and adorned with fresh posters declaring "Make London Manic" and "Ban Beige Politics", hummed with energy. Literally. Someone had left the rooftop speakers playing a loop of jungle remixes, which reverberated against the nearby walls of Westfield Stratford City.

And then came the complaints.

Callie was halfway through a lukewarm can of Cherry Pepsi Max when Tash Crozier appeared, her clipboard clutched tight to her chest and her expression bordering on apocalyptic.

"We've got a situation," she said grimly.

"Another one?" Callie quipped, glancing over from where she was hunched on the top step of the bus. "Is it the thing with the portable loo again? Because I told Kyler not to wedge it behind the Santander Cycles."

"No," Tash replied, eyes flicking toward the crowd starting to gather beyond the railing. "Westfield management have just sent down a rep. They're not happy we're parked here."

Callie stretched her legs. "Bit late for that, innit? We've been here nearly three hours."

"And in that time," Tash said, flipping open her clipboard with a theatrical sigh, "you've hosted a mock debate with DJ Pigeon, spray-painted a slogan across the pavement, and started something that looks a lot like a daytime rave."

Callie tilted her head, as if considering. "Sounds like democracy to me."

Tash gave her a look. "Callie…"

"I know, I know," Callie said, already pulling herself upright and hopping off the bus with a practiced bounce. "Let me guess—they're threatening to call security?"

"They've already called them," said a familiar voice.

Robert Hollis had arrived without fanfare, which for a man as pinstripe and perpetually stern-faced as he was, counted as a grand entrance. He looked like he'd just walked out of a Tory Party reshuffle and into a psychedelic warzone, his expression somewhere between disbelief and resignation.

The fact, Callie knew, was that the Manic Studios, and the Manic Battle Bus, was parked next to the Copper Box Arena, and therefore not on land owned by Westfield itself, but leased by Manic from the London Legacy Development Corporation, the post-Olympics regeneration body that had its fingers in half the East London pie. But that distinction, as Robert Hollis clearly knew, wasn't stopping Westfield's management from making a righteous fuss. Bureaucracy, after all, didn't work on vibes alone.

Robert adjusted his spectacles, his briefcase slung like a weapon beneath one arm. "They've issued a formal notice of complaint. Breach of tenant harmony, obstruction of access, unauthorised event activity, potential licensing violations. You name it."

Callie grinned, brushing a strand of damp hair from her eyes. "You forgot 'general crimes against boring architecture.'"

Robert didn't rise to the bait. "Callie. You're walking a very thin line. Technically we do have the right to occupy this land, but only under the conditions laid out in the LLDC lease. Which—if I may remind you—do not include outdoor sound systems, ad hoc political gatherings, or rave-based diplomacy."

Callie made a grand gesture at the bus, then the cluster of twenty-something onlookers now filming the scene on TikTok. "Robert, look around. This is the most engaged this patch of tarmac has ever been. People are dancing. People are filming. People are vibing. If that's not cultural enrichment, I don't know what is."

Just then, a bass drop from the upper deck sound system triggered a wave of whoops and cheers. DJ Pigeon—still clad in his neon feathered onesie, reflective sunglasses fogged from exertion—poked his head out of the emergency hatch. "Oi Callie! You want jungle or grime next? Crowd's leaning toward grime!"

"Mix it, Pigeon!" Callie yelled back. "We're making a scene, not a playlist!"

A young woman from the Westfield PR team, dressed in black Zara office wear and wielding a laminated ID badge like a dagger, appeared by the railings. She was followed by two burly security guards and a man in an ill-fitting suit who seemed very unsure of why he was there.

"We're going to need you to move your vehicle," the woman called out, trying to make herself heard over the steady throb of the beat. "This is not authorised, and you're in violation of the shopping centre's commercial boundary agreements!"

Callie turned to Robert with a smirk. "Commercial boundary agreements. God, I love it when the suits start talking dirty."

Robert pinched the bridge of his nose. "Do not antagonise them."

Too late.

Callie stepped forward, phone in hand, already livestreaming. "Hello Stratford!" she shouted cheerfully to her growing audience, both digital and physical. "We're coming to you live from the frontlines of the vibes revolution!"

There was an awkward pause from the Westfield rep. "Ms Hall—"

"That's MAYORAL CANDIDATE Hall, if you don't mind," Callie corrected, smiling broadly.

A cheer went up from the crowd, spurred on by DJ Pigeon, who dropped into a remix of Lethal Bizzle's "Pow!" for extra chaos.

Callie continued, now pacing theatrically. "Today, we find ourselves the victims of a heinous injustice. The Manic Battle Bus—a beacon of joy, colour, and extremely questionable parking decisions—is under attack. Why? Because we dared to vibe too hard. Because we dared to bring community, music and colour to a shopping centre beige enough to cause spiritual death."

"This is not public land!" the Westfield rep interjected, but Callie noticed Robert pulled a sheaf of paperwork from his briefcase, turning to the Westfield rep.

"This, madam, states that Manic Radio (London) Ltd is permitted to use the land at Clarnico Lane, London, E20 3AF, bordered by the Copper Box Arena to the north east, Marshgate Lane to the west, the River Lee to the west, Carpenters Lane to the south and Waterden Lane to the north is for the enjoyment and exclusive use by them, their predecessors, successors and any party assigned to them as a contractor, subcontractor or representative. Including—but not limited to—temporary promotional installations, audio demonstrations, community engagement platforms, and public broadcast events. This lease is active until December 31st, 2031."

The Westfield woman blinked, her confidence faltering for a fraction of a second. "Be that as it may," she began, already on the back foot, "your event still constitutes a disturbance."

Robert leaned in, offering a smile that was polite in the most weaponised possible way. "With respect, your concerns may be more properly directed toward the LLDC. We have no obligation to notify Westfield of our activities unless those activities involve direct obstruction of access or incitement of harm. And unless someone's tripped over a fog machine or the bass has physically unseated a Pret A Manger sandwich from a shelf, I believe we are within compliance."

Callie leaned sideways and whispered, not very quietly, "God, Robert's hot when he's legal."

"I heard that," Robert said, expression flat. "And no."

The man in the ill-fitting suit—likely a facilities liaison from Westfield or perhaps a traffic management underling dragged in last minute—cleared his throat and muttered something to the security guards. The taller of the two frowned, obviously unsure of whether they were actually authorised to do anything beyond standing around looking mildly intimidating.

Callie turned back to the crowd, now visibly larger. A few had clearly arrived just to see what the fuss was about, but many had their phones out, livestreaming, posting to stories. She could already imagine the headlines: *Mayoral Candidate Hall in Stand-off with Shopping Centre Over Bass Drops*.

Tash returned with a battered megaphone that looked like it had survived a riot. "Battery's dodgy but it works," she said, thrusting it into Callie's hands.

Callie turned it on and let the static settle before speaking.

"LADIES AND GENTLEMEN," she began, in a booming, dramatically over-enunciated voice. "I stand before you not just as a candidate for Mayor of London, but as a humble defender of fun. The powers that be"— she gestured toward the Westfield lot—"wish to silence us. They wish to sanitise our streets, dull our voices, and remove every last drop of unfiltered joy from the urban sprawl we call home."

A small cheer.

"They claim we are a 'disturbance.' That we 'violate commercial decorum.' I say—sod decorum! We are the future of this city's soul, and we will not be beige-washed into submission!"

This got a bigger cheer. One of the nearby food delivery cyclists stopped pedalling to shout "YES, CALLIE!" before wheeling away down the cycle lane, fist in the air.

And then a police car pulled up.

Two officers emerged, looking as perplexed by the neon spectacle as the Westfield contingent had been. They conferred briefly before approaching Robert, who immediately began a low, earnest conversation, gesturing with his sheaf of papers. Callie couldn't hear the words, but the universal language of legal contention needed no translation. The officers' expressions morphed from confusion to cautious understanding.

Meanwhile, the crowd's energy had pivoted from festive to defiant, the line between public spectacle and public disturbance blurring with every beat that pounded out from DJ Pigeon's deck. Callie knew this delicate dance well—the push and pull of public opinion, the tightrope walk of civil disobedience where one slip could turn a party into a riot or a political statement into a public nuisance charge.

She raised the megaphone to her lips again, her voice ringing clear over the sounds of Stratford. "Friends, Londoners, fellow vibe enthusiasts! Let's show our friends in uniform and our corporate neighbours that our movement is about joy, about community!" She lowered her voice, conspiratorial. "And let's be honest, a bit about annoying the right sort of people."

The officers had finished their discussion with Robert, and one approached Callie, his demeanour not unkind. "Ms. Hall, we appreciate the peaceful nature of your event so far," he began, glancing around as if to make sure peace was still the operative word, "but we've received several complaints about noise and possible traffic disruptions. We need to see some effort to mitigate the disturbance, or we'll have to consider further action."

Callie nodded, her expression sobering under the neon paint streaks across her cheeks. "Understood, officer. We respect the law, even as we challenge the mundane." Turning to the crowd, she clicked off the megaphone and raised her voice naturally. "Alright, everyone! Let's dial down the decibels and move the party inside the bus. We can be a beacon of madness without waking up the whole postcode!"

Her compliance seemed to reassure the police, who lingered as the crowd began to disperse into smaller, more manageable groups, some climbing aboard the bus where the party promised to continue, albeit at a more subdued volume.

As the situation de-escalated, Callie felt a vibration in her pocket. Pulling out her phone, she saw a stream of notifications from social media—clips of her speech, photos of the bus, hashtags like #VibeTheVote and #MakeLondonManic spreading like digital wildfire. She grinned, the potential of viral politics pulsing at her fingertips.

Robert came over, his face a mask of relief and mild irritation. "You handled that well," he admitted, "but we're skating on thin ice here. This kind of stunt pulls attention, but it also pulls scrutiny and the kind of headlines that can swing both ways."

Callie clapped him on the shoulder, feeling the adrenaline of the morning start to ebb. "Robert, my dear, sober strategist, today we didn't just make headlines—we made history. Or at least, we made one hell of a vlog episode."

He didn't smile, but his eyes softened slightly. "Just try to keep the next episode free of police intervention, please."

With the crowd now safely contained and the bus a contained hub of activity, Callie stepped aside to take a call from Tash, who was coordinating the next stop on their guerrilla campaign tour. As she talked, her eyes caught on a young girl in the crowd, her face painted with the Manic logo, watching in awe as DJ Pigeon transitioned the party inside.

It was these moments, Callie realized, that fuelled her campaign—not just the grand gestures or the headline-grabbing antics, but the sparks of inspiration lit in the eyes of the next generation, the potential architects of a more vibrant, more colourful London.

As the conversation wrapped up and she confirmed the next location, Callie looked back at the bus, its garish hues a stark contrast against the drab urban backdrop. It was more than a vehicle; it was a vessel, carrying a motley crew of dreamers, dancers, and doers towards a future where politics was as lively and inclusive as the street art that coloured the city's underpasses.

"On to the next one," she muttered to herself, a smirk playing on her lips as she climbed aboard the bus, the doors closing behind her with a hiss and a promise. The road to City Hall was long and fraught with obstacles, but Callie Hall was ready to drive straight through them, her battle bus blaring all the way.

* _ * _ * _ *

"You're listening to Manic Radio Essex, and we're live from Romford with the Manic Collective Battle Bus," Callie said, as the clock struck 4pm and her show, which she had, despite OFCOM requiring her to stand down as she was an active candidate in the Mayoral election, somehow managed to keep unofficially presenting via pre-recorded "specials" and cleverly labelled outside broadcast segments. It was a legal grey area Robert Hollis had warned her about repeatedly—but in classic Manic fashion, they hadn't so much tiptoed across the line as thrown neon paint at it and used it as a hopscotch grid.

Inside the bus, the broadcast desk was sandwiched between a mini fridge filled with dubious energy drinks, a stack of campaign leaflets featuring DJ Pigeon in a tie, and a DJ deck which Kyler had half-wired into the radio kit with a "this might explode, but vibes" level of confidence.

"Today's topics," Callie continued, voice rich with mock professionalism, "include the fine art of protest through rave, the likelihood of me being arrested before nominations close, and why Romford kebab shops are the unsung heroes of night-time urban resilience."

Jordan sat beside her, reading the latest texts from listeners, one eye twitching from too much Red Bull. "We've had three separate callers offering to get 'Vote Callie' tattoos, one guy wants to marry DJ Pigeon— unclear if he thinks the pigeon is real or a mascot—and someone called 'Gav from Gidea Park' reckons you should take the bus to the Shard and stage a rooftop protest with glow sticks."

"Gav," Callie said solemnly into the mic, "I respect your energy. Also, please don't climb any skyscrapers on my account. Not unless you've got a harness and a lawyer."

Tash appeared at the edge of the broadcast space, her hair in a messy bun, her expression radiating "over it." "We need to talk," she mouthed, and Callie waved Jordan in to vamp for a bit as she ducked behind the curtain draped across the upper deck's back end.

"They're cancelling Brent," Tash whispered. "Council said they won't allow any mobile broadcasts in their public squares. Cited noise pollution and health and safety."

"Health and safety?" Callie hissed. "What, are they worried DJ Pigeon's going to Molotov cocktail a bin?"

Tash smirked despite herself. "They said they don't trust Manic's definition of a 'controlled event.' Honestly, can't blame them."

Callie rubbed her temples. "Alright. What's our next best option?"

Tash pulled out a printed schedule, every line a battlefield of biro scribbles and frantic highlighter marks. "Waltham Forest are still a maybe—if we keep it music-only and don't do speeches. Hackney's already overloaded with events and might throw us out unless we can convince them we're promoting 'creative youth expression.' And Tower Hamlets said yes, but only if we stay near the canal and don't plug anything into street sockets."

"Fine," Callie said. "We'll go guerrilla. Half the charm's in the chaos anyway. Let's roll into Hackney, set up near Broadway Market, keep it spontaneous and low-key."

****

CHAPTER 13 – The Square
Saturday 5th April 2024

The events stage and Battle Bus was parked in Leicester Square, with workers securing the final rigging and the events stage and Battle Bus was parked in Leicester Square, with workers securing the final rigging and threading a sea of garish orange, pink and lime bunting between the lampposts. The Battle Bus gleamed like a neon brick of defiance under the pale spring sunshine, a monument to mischief, pulsing low with bass before the show had even started.

Callie Hall stood at the foot of the stage steps, arms crossed, watching the scene unfold with the air of a general inspecting the front line. Her oversized Manic Collective hoodie was half-zipped over a sequin crop top and flared jeans so wide they looked like they could conceal a small speaker rig. Her hair was piled in a messy bun, streaked with orange and green spray from the previous night's promotional graffiti session in Camden.

"All good with the power feed?" she called over to Wally Penkhirst, one of the electricians who was responsible for ensuring the entire Leicester Square OB didn't blow out a fuse or cause a mass outage of nearby Nando's and souvenir shops. Wally, mid-fifties and shaped like a beer barrel, gave her a thumbs-up while cradling a roll of cable in his other hand.

"Live feed's up and running," he called back in a thick West Ham accent. "If anything shorts, it'll be the Wi-Fi in M&M's World, not us."

Callie snorted. "If we knock the Minstrels offline, we're doing the Lord's work."

She turned back to the Battle Bus just as Daisy bounded down from the upper deck, headphones around her neck and a clipboard in hand.

"We've got twenty-five minutes till London Vibes cuts to us," she said, breathless and buzzing with energy. "OB line's solid. Kyle's doing vox pops up by the Odeon. There's already a queue forming for the free merch, and—get this—we've got an unconfirmed rumour that one of Capital's street team vans did a drive-by to see what we were up to and bailed."

Callie's eyes lit up. "Did anyone get a picture?"

"Yup." Daisy flipped the clipboard to reveal a printed-out still from CCTV footage at the corner of Swiss Court. It clearly showed a grey Global-branded VW van hesitating at the edge of the square, then pulling a swift U-turn back toward Soho.

Callie took the clipboard, holding it up like a trophy. "That is going on our socials. Caption it: 'Even the Empire knows when to retreat.'"

Daisy was already tapping it into her phone. "You're playing a dangerous game, babe."

Callie smirked. "What's the point of revolution if you're not pissing off the right people?"

She turned to face the Battle Bus. Its top deck had been transformed into a DJ booth and pop-up broadcasting suite, kitted with Manic's signature neon signage and a thumping PA system wired through enough amps to start a minor quake. The side panels bore the fresh party emblem: a pigeon in sunglasses spinning decks fashioned from Oyster cards, already immortalised across Twitter and TikTok.

Below, rows of temporary crowd barriers cordoned off a fan zone that was rapidly filling with onlookers. Teens in bucket hats, exhausted parents sipping iced coffee, TikTokers holding ring lights, and the occasional bewildered tourist with a selfie stick—all of them drawn to the curious, carnival-like spectacle.

A banner across the front of the OB desk read: "Make London Fun Again – Live from The Square".

From the corner of her eye, Callie saw Jordan climbing down from the bus, chewing a protein bar and carrying a branded backpack stuffed with merchandise.

"You know Global are going to lose their minds over this, right?" he asked around a mouthful of peanut butter and oats.

"I'm counting on it," Callie said, not missing a beat.

"They've already dispatched a lawyer," he added, pointing out a man in a three piece suit, overcoat, and the look of a KC who Callie knew was Global Media's Head of Legal, in house barrister and King's Council, James Jenkins, along with former Brookes Babe and DEI consultant to the media, Carly Jenkins, who was too busy with her twin children, Oliver and Sebastian, who Callie knew Global had signed to a podcast deal called "Living with Radio's Darth Vader", a tell all podcast about living with a man who was 7 years junior to Ashley Tabor-King, who was close friends with the founder of Global Media and a hereditary peer.

Callie chuckled at how Carly and the teenage twins were more interested in the sound checks than their fathers Legal blistering.

Out of the corner of her eye, she also noticed Nick Ferrari walking into the Global foyer, and then, as sudden as Jenkins had appeared in the Square, he was following Ferrari into the building, phone clamped to his ear and a face like thunder.

A minute later, a text message appeared on her phone, a friend who was a Heart producer.

Helen: Vader is throwing things off his desk up here, and he's cursing your name in Latin. He's even broke his portrait of the King... one that he's had since Charles was crowned. Y'know, he at ATK think Global have a divine right to a monopoly.

Callie stared at the message on her screen for a moment, then turned it to show Daisy, who read it and nearly spat out her sip of flat white.

"Latin?" Daisy wheezed. "He's cursing in Latin?"

Callie smirked. "Well, it is the language of the old elite. Seems only right we rattle them back to their roots."

Helen: He's just submitted an injunction... and now he's cursing his son for saying "the Manic Mayor is hot". Nick

Ferrari is calling it a travesty that the future Lord Jenkins is a teenager with hormones for the wrong person, and that back in his day, men lusted over Thatcher.

Callie had to chuckle at that, especially the dinosaur Nick Ferrari and his outdated notions of acceptable lust objects. She turned the screen so Jordan could see it too, and he let out a bark of laughter that startled a flock of pigeons near the railing.

"Honestly," Jordan said, shaking his head. "If we've got Nick Ferrari lusting over the Iron Lady and you've got a 13 year old Jenkins crushing on you, we've won."

"You know, Jord, I might get the young Ollie Jenkins up here and give him a campaign badge and a microphone," Callie said mischievously. "Imagine the headlines: 'Son of Global Royalty defects to the Manic Revolution.' We'd go viral before lunchtime. That and get him to do a set on the Battle Bus decks."

Jordan almost dropped his protein bar, laughing. "You're dangerous. I love it."

Callie grinned, then snapped into action as the countdown to broadcast hit fifteen minutes. She jogged up the Battle Bus steps two at a time, emerging onto the top deck where the rigged DJ booth overlooked a sea of orange and pink. The Manic Collective's logo was proudly projected onto the surrounding buildings with portable gobos, turning Leicester Square into their own temporary principality of organised rebellion.

Daisy handed her a mic, hot and live on the London Vibes OB feed. She tapped it twice, then leaned into it, her voice ringing out across the Square.

"Alright, London! Welcome to The Square! Welcome to Manic Mayhem! Welcome to... the bloody start of something proper. We are LIVE on London Vibes and Manic Essex, broadcasting not from a sterile glass tower, not from some air-conditioned, focus-grouped radio station, but from the heart of this city, on a Battle Bus covered in graffiti and pigeons with better fashion sense than most politicians!"

The crowd erupted into cheers, phones thrust skyward to capture the moment.

"First up I want to invite a certain teen up to the stage, the star of the new," she said, looking at the note that Jordan had given her, "exclusive podcast on Global Player, 'Living with Radio's Darth Vader', Ollie Jenkins, on to the stage."

Ollie Jenkins, blushing furiously but clearly loving every moment, was ushered towards the steps by Daisy, who clapped him on the back like an old mate sending him into battle. The crowd parted slightly, giving him room to climb up. He wore a London Vibes cap backwards and a Manic Collective hoodie that was slightly too big, sleeves dangling over his hands.

Callie leaned over, handing him the second mic, grinning like a devil on judgement day.

"Ladies and gentlemen," Callie announced to the Square and the two radio feeds, "please give it up for young

Master Jenkins! Son of Global royalty, future Lord of somewhere posh, and, apparently, the most rebellious thirteen-year-old in Leicester Square today!"

The crowd whooped and clapped as Ollie bashfully took the mic. For a second, he looked like he might bolt. But Callie winked at him, and somehow, that tiny moment of encouragement was enough.

He cleared his throat and, in the wobbly voice of a teenage boy mid-puberty, declared:

"VOTE MANIC! GLOBAL IS BORING!"

The eruption of laughter and applause was immediate and immense. Callie doubled over, laughing into her mic. Jordan, Daisy, and even Wally down by the generators were howling. From the upper windows of Global HQ, a few silhouetted figures stared down like disapproving headmasters.

Callie straightened up, wiping a tear from her eye. "Mate, you're a legend," she said, clapping Ollie on the shoulder, before kissing him, taking advantage of his teenage crush. "You've officially done more for democracy today than half the Cabinet."

Callie straightened, still catching her breath from laughter, while Ollie stood there frozen — partly in shock from the kiss, partly in the glow of sudden, roaring approval. His twin brother, Sebastian, could be seen down at the crowd barrier, red-faced, filming the whole thing with the unrestrained glee of someone who knew this would live forever in family WhatsApp groups — and probably the tabloids by morning.

* _ * _ * _ *

"That woman is going to pay for causing this outrage!"

James Jenkins was fuming inside the thick glass walls of Global's Leicester Square headquarters, pacing a track into the pristine marble tiles. His mobile was clamped so tightly to his ear it looked like it might fuse to his head. Across from him, a compliance officer, one of the team whose usual job was to ensure that all legal broadcast rules were adhered to across LBC, Heart and Capital, stood helplessly, clutching a clipboard and nodding miserably.

"Ashley would never permit this... this insolence... from one of his own! And now it's MY son, MY flesh and blood, up there wearing a Manic hoodie like some common TikToker, defiling the reputation of this company!"

The compliance officer – a small, nervous man named Timothy Hales who looked as if he had just stepped out of a law textbook – cleared his throat timidly.

"Sir, with all due respect... young Master Jenkins' actions are... technically outside of broadcast jurisdiction. He wasn't on-air on a Global station, and he's not an employee. We can't file an internal sanction—"

James turned a shade of purple that could have rivalled the bunting strung outside.

"I DON'T WANT SANCTIONS, TIMOTHY, I WANT BLOOD!" he thundered, slamming a fist onto the nearest desk and sending a carefully balanced pile of Heart FM awards tumbling like dominoes. "I want that Battle Bus impounded. I want Callie Hall fined into bankruptcy. I want her banned from the Square, the airwaves, and preferably the country! I want a new portrait to of His Majesty on my bloody wall by Monday, and I want whoever thought it was a good idea to give her a platform sacked, flogged, and blackballed from media for life!"

Loading up his computer, James pulled his template that he used to sue Manic or Bauer, the templates he used to force them into wars of attrition, to make them lose, to make them pay Global damages and costs for daring to stand against the monopoly he saw as his birthright. His fingers rattled over the keyboard, drafting the injunction with the speed and bitterness of a man who had spent two decades weaponizing paperwork.

"Oh, and Timothy, tell Carly I'll get the train home, she and the kids can take the Bentley. Or better yet, book some tickets to the West End for something Ollie and Seb will love, get them out of this square before I have to call in the security myself. I can't deal with the bloody optics of my own family on TikTok wearing the enemy's colours!"

Timothy, clutching his clipboard like a life preserver, scurried off without another word, dodging fallen awards and a bewildered intern carrying a tray of flat whites. James turned back to his computer, growling under his breath as he attached the hastily drafted injunction notice to an email titled: "URGENT - Legal Action Against Manic Radio".

James knew that this wasn't the first time that he had taken on Manic. Nor would it be the last. But this time—this time it was personal.

He hit Send with the force of a man launching a missile, sat back in his chair, and tried to pretend he hadn't just witnessed his own thirteen-year-old heir effectively defect to the enemy live on two radio feeds, half of TikTok, and God knows how many tourist livestreams from the square.

* _ * _ * _ *

Callie passed the mic back to Daisy, who was now grinning so broadly it looked like her face might split in half.

"Well, folks," Daisy said into the mic, bouncing lightly on her toes, "if you're just tuning in — welcome to *history*. We're turning Leicester Square into a carnival of chaos, love, politics, and seriously questionable fashion choices."

Callie laughed, grabbing a can of Monster from the Battle Bus mini fridge and cracking it open with a theatrical flourish. Jordan bounded up next to her, a GoPro mounted on his forehead.

"Right," he panted. "Street team's ready. Kez is bringing the petition boards down now. We've got the merch boxes. And Sticky's on his way with the portable graffiti wall."

Callie's eyes lit up. "Sticky's coming?!"

Jordan nodded. "Yeah, he's got a twelve-foot stretch of blank boarding and about thirty cans of neon paint. Says he's planning to recreate the DJ pigeon 'but, like, if it went clubbing for three days and forgot where its nest was.' His words."

"Perfect," Callie beamed. "The chaos expands."

Sure enough, moments later, Shaun "Sticky" Willis — Manic's unofficial graffiti artist-in-residence and chaos goblin — came pushing a massive roll of white boarding through the square, a shopping trolley rattling behind him absolutely stuffed with paint cans.

He wore a battered denim jacket covered in patches, Doc Martens scuffed to death, and a grin that screamed 'public nuisance in progress'.

"Alright, you reprobates," Sticky yelled over the bass thudding from the Battle Bus. "Where d'you want it?"

"Centre stage, baby!" Callie shouted back, pointing to a space just by the fan barriers. "Let the public have a go too. Spray your slogan, your dream, your rage — whatever. One rule though—"

—"Make it loud, make it proud, and no drawing dicks bigger than Big Ben, alright?" Jordan continued with a wink.

The crowd roared with laughter, some already pushing forward eagerly, phones held aloft, while Sticky grinned and set to work anchoring the makeshift graffiti wall. Volunteers from the Manic Collective street team fanned out around him, handing out cans of spray paint like candy on Halloween.

Callie watched it all unfold from the Battle Bus top deck: the neon bunting fluttering, the impromptu art session beginning, Jordan livestreaming like a possessed influencer, Daisy hyping up the mic with a rolling commentary of the best slogans being sprayed.

Within minutes, the wall blossomed into a riot of colour and slogans:

- **"FREE THE PIGEONS"**

- **"VOTE CHAOS"**

- **"BURN THE BORING"**

- **"NO MORE SAFE SEATS, ONLY DANCEFLOORS"**

Even a pensioner in a tweed coat and walking stick was having a crack, carefully painting **"I HATE BORING POLITICS"** in wobbly letters before posing for a photo with a pair of grinning teenagers.

Callie felt a fizzing, unstoppable grin spread across her face as she stood atop the Battle Bus and watched her revolution come to life.

This — this chaotic fusion of street art, raves, kids on scooters, teens livestreaming, old ladies painting protest slogans — *this* was the spirit she wanted to inject back into London politics. Not sterile manifesto launches in glass towers. Not dreary speeches at the Royal Festival Hall to a crowd of interns and lobbyists. *This.*

Down on the square, the graffiti wall was now a swirling tapestry of neon anarchy. Someone had drawn a giant pigeon wearing a crown, flanked by the words *MAKE LONDON YOURS*. Someone else had scrawled *NO MORE RADIO ZOMBIES* in messy orange letters that dripped like wet paint tears.

Sticky, still darting around like an excitable Jack Russell, had managed to tag *VOTE CALLIE – FREE THE DLR* in three separate places without anyone noticing until Daisy pointed it out, howling with laughter.

Behind her, the bass dropped into a new track — an original Manic remix of *London Calling* by The Clash, distorted and turbocharged with an EDM beat that rattled the windows of the Leicester Square Wetherspoons.

Callie raised her arms theatrically over her head, letting the crowd's energy wash over her. Hundreds of people packed into the fan zone now, and more were spilling in from the surrounding streets, drawn by the noise, the colour, the sheer lawless fun of it all.

At the back of the crowd, Jordan and the street team were handing out Manic Collective flags, hastily printed flyers ("*Vote Callie — Because Beige is Boring*") and clipboards to start gathering nomination signatures.

"Alright!" Callie shouted into the mic, her voice soaring over the thumping bassline. "You lot want a London that's alive, that's messy, that's yours? Then get your arses over to the street team, sign your borough's sheet, and make it bloody happen!"

The cheer that erupted was near-deafening. Callie laughed again, throwing up a peace sign, her sequin top flashing in the sun like a disco ball.

Daisy bounded up beside her, mic still hot, and leaned in. "You've got, like, sixty signatures already from just three boroughs. This is insane."

Callie beamed, handing the mic back to Daisy and grabbing her Monster for another long swig. "Insane is the point. We're breaking the script."

As Daisy hyped the crowd into more dancing and chanting, Callie hopped off the Battle Bus top deck and darted back into the thick of it, weaving through the crowd to Sticky's impromptu graffiti workshop.

A kid no older than ten was standing on tiptoes to spray *BAN BORING COUNCILS* in shaky pink letters. His mum, laughing helplessly, held the can steady for him.

Sticky clapped him on the back. "First political act sorted, mate. You're gonna go far."

Callie crouched down next to the boy, handing him a Manic badge. "Stick this on your rucksack, kid. You'll be cooler than half your headteachers by Monday."

He beamed at her, tucking the badge proudly into his pocket.

She stood, brushing neon dust off her jeans, and surveyed the scene: pure, untamed civic joy.

And then, of course, the police arrived.

It wasn't a full raid — no sirens, no riot shields — but two Met PCSOs in high-vis jackets pushed their way carefully through the crowd towards the Battle Bus.

Jordan spotted them first. "We've got rozzers, two o'clock," he muttered into the wireless earpiece they all wore.

"Relax," Callie murmured back. "It's legal. Ish."

The officers — a woman in her thirties with an unimpressed squint, and a gangly young guy who looked about fifteen — approached the barrier.

Callie intercepted them, all bright smiles and open arms.

"Afternoon, officers!" she chirped. "Beautiful day for democracy, isn't it?"

The female officer gave her a look that could have wilted the bunting.

"We've had a report of unlicensed events and obstruction," she said in a tone that suggested she'd rather be anywhere else.

Callie pulled out a battered manila folder from the Battle Bus steps and handed over a sheaf of papers — permits, noise assessments, crowd control plans. All properly rubber-stamped after two weeks of Robert Hollis' meticulous, soul-crushing legal prep.

"Everything's legit, boss," she said cheerfully. "OB license granted, public engagement permit secured via Westminster Council, sound levels pre-approved, and street team briefed on public order compliance. We're even handing out free earplugs."

The young male PCSO blinked at her in awe, clearly overwhelmed.

The woman, after scanning the paperwork with a professional eye, sighed heavily and nodded.

"Fine," she said. "But if you block the pedestrian routes or cause a stampede, it's on you."

"Wouldn't dream of it," Callie said sweetly. "We're more chaos with consent, you know?"

The officers retreated, and Callie immediately raised both fists triumphantly towards the Battle Bus.

"We're good!" she yelled, and a fresh roar from the crowd echoed off the surrounding buildings.

****

CHAPTER 14 – Injunction Junction
Tuesday 9th April 2024

The day began not with a bang, but a knock — the kind of sharp, officious knock that sets every stomach in a ten-metre radius tumbling into their trainers.

Callie Hall, groggy-eyed and half-covered in a duvet with the words VOTE CHAOS sprayed across it in neon pink, sat up too fast and promptly whacked her head on the low ceiling of her Romford bedroom. The ceiling, for some random reason Callie couldn't work out, seemed lower than usual. Maybe it was a result of the all-nighter she'd just pulled, or perhaps the universe was aligning to tell her she'd made a terrible mistake about her choice of venue for the previous night's DIY graffiti session. Either way, her skull was about to make some serious arguments with the plaster.

"Fffff—!" Callie hissed, rubbing the top of her head as she staggered up and reached for her phone. As expected, a flurry of messages and notifications awaited her, lighting up the screen with chaotic fervour.

She glanced at the time. 8:47 AM. She was supposed to be awake for at least the past hour, yet the Battle Bus escapades had kept her up until almost four in the morning, glued to her phone, firing off press releases, responding to an avalanche of social media comments, and dealing with frantic team members asking if they could get more pigeons into the campaign.

Another knock sounded, this time much louder.

"Bloody hell, who's that?" Callie groaned, pushing the duvet off herself. She gave her hair a dishevelled tug, muttered an assortment of profanity, and finally trudged to the door, still in her slippers, still half-dressed in last night's battle attire—her "official" look for the campaign being a Manic Collective hoodie and shorts that were far too revealing for a Monday morning.

She yanked open the door, half-expecting to see one of her erratic, overly energetic street team members, or one of her fellow chaos merchants—perhaps Daisy, running late for something. But, no. Standing in the doorway was the postman, his shorts looking, to Callie, as if he were packing more than the usual parcels and a grin which, in her cocaine addled mind, meant that he was either giving her the eye, or a stripogram that Daisy had ordered as a joke. Either way, Callie blinked twice before she remembered how to form words.

"Morning gorgeous. I've got a... special delivery... for you," he chirped, and Callie could swear she saw him wink at her.

She looked down at his shorts again and realised, with a dawning sense of betrayal, that she might still be tripping slightly from the fumes of the neon paint used on Sticky's portable graffiti wall the night before. Shaking the mental glitter out of her ears, she rubbed her eyes and tried to focus.

The "special delivery" turned out to be a heavy envelope, thick with the kind of legal heft that only a city law firm can conjure up — expensive, embossed, and smug.

"Cheers," Callie muttered, taking it with exaggerated suspicion.

"No worries, Miss Hall," said the postman, tipping an invisible cap and walking off down the steps. Callie closed the door with her foot, muttering "bloody theatre students moonlighting as postmen," and tore the envelope open.

She didn't need to finish reading the first paragraph before she got the gist.

She, as one of 20 respondents in one single case, along with Daisy, Sticky, Kyler, Jordan, Manic Radio Group Ltd, Manic Vibes Ltd, Manic Ventures Ltd, Manic Essex Radio Ltd, and Manic Properties Ltd amongst others, including 'persons unknown', were 'kindly invited', aka summoned, to the High Court, for a preliminary injunction hearing. Not next week. Not tomorrow. In three hours.

Even Robert Hollis, Manic's laconic, terrifyingly efficient Head of Legal, Richard Hammond, the driver of the battle bus, and the Financial Director of Manic Radio, Dennis Drummond, were named, as well as the CEO, Adam Banks, and, surprisingly, Sheikh Al-Mahmoud al-Fazari, the owner of Manic Radio, as a respondent.

"Fucking hell. How the fuck did he get dragged into this?" Callie muttered, staring at the Sheikh's name as if it had materialised via some ancient curse rather than legal paperwork. "He's in Dubai. I don't even think he knows we have a bus."

Grabbing her phone, she noticed that there was a WhatsApp in the Stratford Hub Chat, a group that all Manic hosts, producers and technicians who were based at the Olympic Park studios, from Kyler, who was presenting his Manic Radio South Coast breakfast show on location from Brighton, all the way to Tash Crozier, who ran events and was currently sleeping under a trestle table at the back of the Manic Warehouse, had been spamming since 7:30am.

Kyler Thompson: *JENKINS HAS GONE FULL NUCLEAR.*

Daisy Round: *What the ACTUAL HELL is this? Just got served at my mum's house??*

Jordan McCabe: *Anyone else just get hit with 12kg of legal paper?*

Tash Crozier: *Guys, someone wake Callie up NOW. I've just spoken to Rob Hollis. He's already at the court.*

Laurence Kendal: *I'm not a fall guy but I do have fake IDs if it comes to that.*

Callie fired off a voice note before she even made it to the kettle.

"Right. Everyone breathe. I've got the notice. It's mad, it's dramatic, it's peak Jenkins, but it's also public record, which means it's now content. Meet me at the High Court by 11:30. Dress loud. Bring cameras. If we're gonna get sued, we're gonna trend doing it."

She tossed the phone onto her bed, then peeled off her campaign hoodie in favour of an even louder one—acid yellow with "FREE THE BUS" across the front. She threw on sunglasses (indoors, naturally), grabbed the rest of her cold Monster from the floor, and stuffed the injunction papers into her oversized pigeon-print tote bag.

The Manic Battle Bus might've been banished from Leicester Square, but she wasn't going down without a very loud, very online fight.

* _ * _ * _ *

"It's nine o'clock on Manic Radio Surrey, and coming up after the news, some of our colleagues have been summoned by the Overlord of Global Media, Lord James Edward Jenkins KC, yes, the killjoy who wants to take your pigeons, your Battle Bus, and possibly your soul if you play music that isn't beige enough."

Looking round the kitchen of his Henley-on-Thames manor that had been in the Jenkins family for generations, James Jenkins did not smile at the sound of his own name being butchered on Manic Radio Surrey. In fact, he scowled so hard that his forehead creased into a grid pattern sharp enough to qualify as a topographical map.

He stood stiffly in his granite-and-chrome kitchen, holding a Fortnum & Mason teacup in one hand and the Financial Times in the other, the latter trembling just slightly with fury. He had been up since dawn—partly out of habit, partly because he hadn't been able to sleep after the events in Leicester Square had become the talk of every newsroom from Newsnight to Good Morning Britain.

The Battle Bus had been a theatrical violation of everything he believed media ought to be: well-ordered, immaculately branded, and firmly under control. Instead, he'd watched his own son—his heir, no less—stand beside a woman who treated civic procedure like an improv sketch and scream "GLOBAL IS BORING" into a microphone before half of TikTok.

He set the teacup down with the delicacy of a man who had once interned at Buckingham Palace, then pulled out his phone and flicked through the barrage of alerts. Legal injunction granted. Social media exploding. #LetTheBusPark was trending number one in the UK, second worldwide behind #ZaynAndGigiBackTogether.

And now, to add insult to catastrophic injury, Callie Hall had turned it into a brand.

There were T-shirts already. Stickers. Pop-up ads on YouTube. Someone had projected "LET THE BUS PARK YOU COWARDS" across the BBC Broadcasting House overnight.

"Well, you've made yourself popular, James," his wife, Carly, said, groaning at the radio broadcast that was playing in the background of the kitchen. "Thank goodness the twins are spending the day with the family of The Viscount Camrose and his children, and not-"

James noticed Carly look at the piece of paper that was on the desk, which he had written, a summons for Oliver as a witness for the defence, and for the Crown if necessary.

James crossed the room in two long, stormy strides and snatched the sheet from the countertop before Carly could finish reading. Her eyes, already narrowed, followed his movements like a hawk.

"You were going to make him testify?" she asked, voice low and dangerous.

"He's thirteen," James snapped. "He doesn't get to stand on stages declaring treason against his father's company and waltz away like it's a bloody school play."

Carly folded her arms. "So you're going to drag him into court to prove what? That your pride matters more than your family?"

James didn't answer immediately. Instead, he turned towards the marble kitchen island, palms flat against the surface, head bowed. The silence hung, thick with consequence. Finally, he exhaled through his nose like a dragon holding in fire.

"Ashley, Michael, my father and I built Global from-"

"No, James, you didn't build Global. You were Ashley's spy in GCap, learning law from the operational side and reporting back like a bloody Edwardian hall monitor," Carly snapped. "You've made a career out of being a legal bully in bespoke tailoring, suing everyone, from hospital radio to Bauer and Radio Jackie for playing 'Bohemian Like You' too many times. Don't pretend you're some visionary. You're a compliance officer with delusions of empire. You know, some days I wish that I'd never shagged you when we were at Uni, or signed up to that Brookes Babe shit."

James' face stiffened, but the muscles in his jaw betrayed him with a twitch. His reputation had been forged in polished boardrooms and mahogany courtrooms, not domestic stand-offs on marble tiles. But Carly had always had the ability to strike deeper than any legal adversary, and today, she came armed with truth, not threats.

"Well piss off back to Chelmsford then," James snarled, instantly regretting the words as they left his mouth. "I... I... I mean, I shouldn't have said that. Look... I'll... I'll make it right. Just—don't make this personal when it already is. You think I want to drag Ollie into court? If I don't defend Global's interests, then Ashley will think I'm weak. He'll think I'm no longer the man he needs to run legal. He'll cling on to Global and then I won't get what I'm owed, as I'm meant to be the heir apparent. This isn't just about Callie bloody Hall. This is about legacy. Mine. Ours. Do you think I really wanted to be this ruthless, be a cold hearted bastard who sues a heart ward for playing George Michael without clearance? No. But I did it because Ashley corrupted me, made me into the fucking machine he wanted. Some days, when I'm driving home, I'm in fucking tears because I'm ashamed of what I've become."

The confession hung in the air like a rogue broadcast—raw, unscripted, and impossible to take back.

Carly stared at him. There was no victory in her face, only sadness. "Then why are you still playing the villain, James?" she asked quietly. "If you hate it so much, why are you still swinging the axe?"

"Because if I don't, Carter fucking Ruck will. They'll swoop in, take my job, take my office, and next thing I know I'll be reduced to a footnote in Global's annual report—'Jenkins, James. Retired under pressure.' I built a kingdom out of red tape, Carly. If I let this chaos circus win—if I let Callie Hall turn my son into a meme and my company into a punchline—I lose everything. Do you know why I volunteer to do cover shifts on Radio X?"

James's voice cracked slightly, the hard edge in his words giving way to something unexpectedly human. He looked at Carly, his eyes wet with exhaustion.

"Because for three hours on a Saturday night, when no one's listening, I get to be someone else. I sit there, spinning Joy Division and New Order, pretending I'm not the man who once sued a hospice radio station over Ed Sheeran. I get to go back to those Sundays that you and I did the cover shifts on Brookes Vibes, whenever Big Bam was off sick, and we'd fuck around, taking the piss out of every song and pretending we were anarchists with a transmitter. Anyway, part of my vendetta against Manic nowadays... it's because of Banks. That bastard who ran the promotions team when we were at Brookes Vibes, the bastard who allowed Annabelle to force me into that van in 2003 back in Banbury when we were doing that promo for Banbury Beats, when she cornered me... and I said no.

* - * - * - *

Saturday 29th November 2003

Carly had never been one for office politics, but when it came to Annabelle Young, she was starting to reconsider.

For weeks, the tension between them had been growing, simmering beneath the surface of every team meeting, promo run, and passive-aggressive email conversation between the Oxford and the Brookes university students.

And then it all came to a head earlier that day.

Annabelle had, while she, Carly, Clarissa and James had been on a promo run on loan to the Banbury Beats station, pulled the ultimate power move.

She had dragged James into the Babemobile and tried to sleep with him. In broad daylight in Banbury town centre.

James had tried to resist, tried to extricate himself from the situation with some semblance of dignity, but Annabelle wasn't one to take no for an answer—especially when she was playing a game she was determined to win.

Carly had found out in the worst way possible.

She and Clarissa had been handing out promo flyers outside a café, chatting away about the upcoming Brookes Vibes Christmas party, when Mark had come jogging up to them, slightly out of breath, eyes wide with alarm.

"You need to get to the Babemobile. Now," he had panted, hands on his knees.

Carly had shared a look with Clarissa before setting off at a determined pace, her boots clicking against the pavement. She knew Annabelle had been up to something all afternoon—she'd been smug, smirking every time Carly so much as glanced in her direction.

And now, as Carly stormed towards the van, she realised why.

She flung the door open without thinking, her stomach already twisted in knots, and found Annabelle naked as the day she was born, and James's erection in Anabelle's quim, him trying to force her off while Annabelle was bouncing on top of him like a jockey on a racehorse.

For a second, the whole world seemed to slow down.

The sound of the bustling Banbury high street faded into nothing. Carly's brain refused to process what she was seeing—Annabelle, stark naked, riding James like her life depended on it, her manicured nails digging into his shoulders, her head thrown back in mock ecstasy.

James, for his part, looked like he was having the worst day of his life. His hands were on Annabelle's hips, but not in a way that suggested enthusiasm—more like he was actively trying to push her off him while she clung on like a stubborn limpet.

"Carly—" James started, his voice sharp with panic, but it was too late.

Carly saw red.

Without thinking, she lunged forward, grabbing Annabelle by the hair and yanking her backwards with a force that sent her sprawling onto the floor of the van. Annabelle let out a yelp, scrambling to cover herself with one of the discarded promo t-shirts that had been lying around.

*"What the fuck do you think you're doing?" Carly spat,
her Essex accent making a full comeback in her fury. "You
desperate, slimy little rat!"*

*Annabelle, ever the actress, plastered an expression of
faux innocence across her face. "Oh, Carly," she panted,
adjusting the shirt over her chest like she was the victim
here. "I thought you knew about our little arrangement.
James and I have been... reconnecting." She smirked,
knowing exactly what she was doing. "He's been
struggling, poor thing, and I thought I'd offer some...
stress relief."*

*Seeing red, Carly dragged Annabelle out of the Ford
Transit, off the mattress, onto the ground, and, seeing the
ironically placed mud pit that Adam had hired, decided
that Annabelle needed a lesson in humility.*

*With a sharp shove, Carly sent Annabelle stumbling
backwards into the thick, sludgy mud that had been left
behind from the morning's promo stunt. Annabelle let out
a high-pitched shriek as she landed on her arse, her bare
legs coated in filth, her perfectly curled blonde hair now
streaked with brown.*

*Clarissa, who had just arrived at the scene, burst out
laughing. "Oh my God, Carly, you legend!" she cackled,
clutching her stomach.*

*James, who had managed to yank his jeans back up with
lightning speed, ran a hand through his dishevelled hair,
looking as though he'd rather be anywhere else in the
world. "Carly, for fuck's sake—"*

"Oh, don't you Carly me, Jenkins!" she snapped, rounding on him. "What the fuck was that? You think I'm some sort of mug? Letting her climb on you like you're some kind of fairground ride?"

James groaned, rubbing his temples. "I wasn't letting her do anything, Carly! You think I wanted this? She just—" He gestured helplessly towards the still-spluttering Annabelle, who was now frantically trying to wipe mud from her face while looking around for help. "She jumped on me! I literally told her to get off—what part of that wasn't clear?!"

James groaned, rubbing his temples. "I wasn't letting her do anything, Carly! You think I wanted this? She just—" He gestured helplessly towards the still-spluttering Annabelle, who was now frantically trying to wipe mud from her face while looking around for help. "She jumped on me! I literally told her to get off—what part of that wasn't clear?! Look, if I wasn't serious about you, do you think I would have taken you to meet my bloody parents?"

Carly's glare didn't soften, though the mention of their recent trip to Henley did briefly flash through her mind. James had been serious about her, hadn't he? He wouldn't have put her through that whole ordeal with his aristocratic father and his laid back but posh mother if he didn't actually care. But that didn't erase the fact that Annabelle had been naked on top of him like some desperate homewrecker from Hollyoaks.

Annabelle, still sitting in the mud with a face like a slapped arse, flipped her wet hair over her shoulder, her smirk returning despite her absolute state. "Oh, please," *she scoffed. "Carly, babes, don't act like you're shocked. Did you really think he was gonna settle for a girl from Essex when he could have me? I mean, look at him—look at me." She gestured to her mud-covered body, as if that somehow strengthened her case.*

Slap.

Carly's hand acted without thinking, the crack of palm against cheek ringing out loud and clear over the stunned silence that had fallen over the promo team. Annabelle's head snapped to the side, her smirk vanishing in an instant.

The next thing Carly knew, however, was the pull of two people grabbing her and dragging her off Annabelle, the click of handcuffs, the cold bite of steel wrapped around her wrists. A sharp voice cut through the stunned silence.

"All right, that's enough! You're coming with us."

Carly blinked, her breath still coming fast as she processed what was happening. Two police officers—both looking unimpressed, both wearing the telltale fluorescent yellow vests—were now holding onto her arms, firmly but not aggressively. One of them, a stocky bloke in his forties with a gruff Midlands accent, was already pulling her towards the waiting panda car.

James was the first to snap out of his shock. "Wait— what? Officer, this isn't—" He ran a hand through his already-messy hair, looking half-dressed and entirely panicked.

"She attacked me!" Annabelle shrieked from the mud, her posh accent wobbling with faux distress. "Did you see that? She assaulted me! I want her charged!"

"Oh, she's not the only one being arrested," another police officer said, and Carly noticed a grin on her face as she pulled her handcuffs out and tried to grab Annabelle, who was resisting as if her life depended on it.

"Oh, no fucking way!" Annabelle shrieked, scrambling to her feet, slipping on the mud as she tried to dodge the officer's grasp. "I'm the victim here! She attacked me! Arrest her, not me!"

The officer, a woman in her early thirties with sharp eyes and an even sharper smirk, didn't look the least bit impressed. "You were stark naked in a public place in the middle of Banbury town centre, miss. That's an indecent exposure charge. Now, are you gonna come quietly, or are we adding resisting arrest to the list?"

* _ * _ * _ *

Tuesday 9th April 2024

In a second-hand Ford Transit with a barely functional heater, Callie and Daisy were racing through Holborn in traffic that moved like treacle and sounded like a headache.

"Jesus Christ, the traffic's worse than Kez's playlist," Daisy muttered, hanging out the passenger window to shout at a Deliveroo cyclist. "Oi! You wanna swap wheels?"

Callie, hunched behind the wheel in oversized sunglasses and a hoodie so bright it could be seen from the ISS, simply grinned. "No stress. Rob says they'll delay the hearing start slightly. Reckons Jenkins requested it himself so his tie could be steamed."

"Because of course he did," Daisy deadpanned, fishing through her bag for lip balm and finding, instead, a rogue campaign badge, a half-eaten Curly Wurly, and a flyer that simply read 'Let the Bus Park, You Cowards!' in gothic font. "Are we seriously walking into the High Court like this?"

Callie flicked on the indicators and swerved around a bin lorry. "Mate, we're not just walking in. We're staging a bloody media moment."

"Please tell me you haven't turned this into another TikTok," Daisy said, already knowing the answer.

"I uploaded a teaser with a 90s rave remix of Law & Order's theme about an hour ago. It's already got 42k likes."

Daisy stared at her. "You're unreal."

"No," Callie smirked. "I'm unelectable. There's a difference. Anyway, you know the boss used to be Jenkins's boss once."

"Wait, what?" Daisy gaped. "Adam Banks? Our Adam? Like... Manic Radio CEO, always-wearing-a-gilet, drinks oat lattes, that Adam Banks?"

Callie grinned wider as she brought the van to a stop outside the High Court. "Yep. Back in the day. When Jenkins was a runner. Banks had him do promos in really tight trunks and mud wrestling in Oxford city centre for Brookes Vibes back in 2003. There's photos somewhere. Best thing is, his wife, Carly, that bitch who forced us to do that EDI seminar at the last all-hands, was a Brookes Babe. She was one of the promo girls in slutty short skirts and crop tops who was involved in the mud wrestling stunt. And get this—he's the one who got her in the Babes, as Banksy apparently told him that she was hired without even an interview because she was his friend and occasional, at the time, shag. Banksy is full of stories from his Trent FM and Brookes Vibes days when you get him downing a few pints. Anyway, he reckons Jenkins never got over it — spent the next two decades turning himself into some walking OFCOM compliance manual just to prove he was better than the mud and the Manic."

Daisy let out a long, low whistle. "No wonder he's trying to shut us down. It's not just about politics or permits. It's about petty revenge from a man who once had to wrestle in neon shorts for a pint and a byline."

"And now," Callie said, stepping out of the van and slinging her pigeon-print tote over one shoulder, "he's up against the ghost of Banbury mud past."

****

CHAPTER 15 - Pigeons Over Parliament

Monday 15th April 2024

It had been a week since the Royal Courts of Justice had declared that Global Media could gain an injunction against "unauthorised static or mobile broadcast installations" within designated high-footfall areas—Leicester Square, Oxford Circus, and anywhere within 500 metres of Parliament Square. The legalese was thick enough to choke a barrister, but the intention was clear: no more Battle Bus. No more pop-up DJ decks. No more spray-painted slogans or sticky-fingered street teams rallying the youth into the kind of dance-fuelled defiance that made James Jenkins' temples throb.

That, of course, the next day, was, with the Permission of the Court, stayed, meaning that pending appeal, Callie could still do pretty much whatever the hell she wanted— as long as it didn't involve permanent structures, amplified music after 8pm, or, apparently, inflatables larger than a Ford Fiesta.

Which was precisely why, at 10:04 AM on Monday, 15th April 2024, Callie Hall was standing in a pigeon onesie, microphone clipped to the hood, livestreaming on six platforms from the footpath of Westminster Bridge with a small trebuchet-like contraption constructed from reclaimed scaffolding poles and the gutted insides of a pressure washer.

She wasn't alone.

Next to her, Jordan McCabe, her long-suffering producer and chaos co-pilot, was wearing a hi-vis vest emblazoned with Pigeon Logistics Coordinator. His job, ostensibly, was to stop anyone from mistaking the machine for a weapon—or worse, something functional. He had already been approached three times that morning by concerned tourists asking if it was an art installation. He had just started saying yes.

And rounding out the trio was DJ Pigeon—the now-iconic campaign mascot and part-time performance artist. Also known today as Tash in a feathered balaclava and glitter trainers, DJ Pigeon was bobbing along to a Bluetooth speaker that, crucially, complied with every single decibel limitation imposed by the High Court's interim ruling. The beats were mellow enough to pass for ambient noise, but punchy enough to form a soundscape of gentle rebellion.

A modest crowd had begun to gather on the bridge, a motley assortment of Manic Collective faithfuls, tourists confused but delighted by the spectacle, and a few political observers with notepads, muttering into iPhones. Ella Booth, Manic Radio's political correspondent, had arrived early in a bright red beret and aviators, reporting live for their on-air news bulletin.

"And in today's top story," she declared to her listeners, standing just metres from Big Ben, "Callie Hall is once again defying the gravity of conventional politics—and, possibly, several bits of health and safety legislation. This time, she's launching biodegradable pigeon-shaped confetti across the Thames in what she claims is a 'message of freedom, rebellion, and eco-conscious

212

silliness.' Critics say it's performance art masquerading as policy. Her supporters say... well, they're wearing pigeon hats and cheering."

Callie gave a theatrical bow to the smartphone cameras lined up on the bridge's railings and leaned into her mic.

"Morning, London! Or should I say... morning to all the ministers, mandarins and millionaires in Parliament, hiding behind their iron gates and sterile soundbites. We're here today because politics is too beige, too bland, and frankly, too scared of glitter. So we're delivering a little joy, a little mess—and a whole flock of biodegradable mischief—right to the doorstep of the mother of all parliaments."

She turned to Jordan. "Status of the payload?"

Jordan, consulting a clipboard with exaggerated gravity, gave a sharp nod. "Flock is armed. Wind vector favourable. Trajectory clear."

Callie spun on her heel, arms aloft. "Then let the pigeons fly!"

The small trebuchet gave a satisfyingly comedic whump, and from it soared a burst of biodegradable pigeon silhouettes—gliding in every direction like tiny paper doves fleeing a confetti cannon at a rave. The sun caught them mid-arc, giving the illusion of a thousand fluttering symbols of joy—and minor administrative nuisance— dancing over the Thames.

Tourists clapped. A baby squealed with delight. A suited civil servant walking towards the Parliamentary estate did a visible double take and muttered "Bloody hell" into his takeaway flat white.

"Message delivered!" shouted Callie, raising her arms like a triumphant general. "This is not just a campaign. It's a feathered revolution!"

From somewhere behind her, DJ Pigeon let out a perfectly timed squawk over the speaker system, followed by a sample from London Calling that had been just trimmed enough to avoid licensing infringement.

At that moment, a cab door opened across the road near Portcullis House, and out stepped an unlikely ally: Lord Alfie Gold, independent peer, eccentric old radical, and owner of more novelty waistcoats than there were working lifts in Parliament.

He was wearing one such waistcoat now—purple velvet with gold brocade—and atop his head sat a bowler hat customised with tiny clock hands, all pointing to 'NOW'.

"Marvellous show!" he called across the road, waving a battered copy of The Guardian like a fan at Glastonbury. "You're a necessary nuisance, Miss Hall! A parliamentary pox on bureaucratic boredom!"

Callie blinked in disbelief as he made his way towards them, clutching a thermos labelled 'GIN (NOT TEA)' and beaming like a schoolboy bunking off Latin.

"Lord Gold," she said, pulling off her pigeon hood to shake his hand. "Didn't expect to see you on the bridge."

"Well, I came out to vote down a digital ID bill," he said, squinting at the sky. "Then I heard someone was launching pigeons over Parliament and thought, 'Alfie, your Monday just improved.' You know, in 1968 I climbed Nelson's Column in protest against motorway signage. Never trust a man who believes Helvetica is the answer to civic engagement."

Callie tried to stifle a snort. Jordan failed entirely.

"Miss Hall," Lord Gold continued, planting his cane into the tarmac like a sceptre. "What you're doing here is important. Performance is power. Symbols are subversion. And frankly, I've sat through enough Lords' debates this year to know that the place needs a damn good pigeoning."

Ella Booth, microphone still recording, stepped closer. "Lord Gold, do you support Miss Hall's candidacy for Mayor of London?"

He stroked his chin thoughtfully. "Support may be too sterile a term. I applaud her. I admire her. I might even vote for her if she promises to abolish the concept of compulsory neckties."

"Done," Callie grinned. "You can write it into the next Act of Vibes."

Lord Gold twirled his cane in a slow, thoughtful loop. "Splendid. Then consider me provisionally on board. And in the spirit of shared nonsense—" he handed Callie a small velvet pouch "—I brought these from my days in the Department for Creative Resistance."

She opened it, revealing an assortment of enamel pins, each shaped like miniature protest placards with slogans such as *Ban Boredom*, *Vive La Vibe*, and *Reclaim the Rave*. Without hesitation, she chose one reading *Power to the Pigeons* and pinned it to the front of her pigeon onesie, just above her campaign rosette.

Jordan glanced at his phone and winced. "Heads up. Someone from the Commons just rang the studio. They're not thrilled."

"No," Ella chimed in, checking her own device, "but they're not arresting anyone either. Word from the Serjeant at Arms' office is 'deeply unimpressed, but technically within bounds of the permit.' They're issuing a mild scolding via formal letter."

Callie grinned. "A scolding? From the hallowed halls of Westminster? That's practically a love letter."

Just then, a jogger passed by, slowed, did a double take, and said breathlessly, "Are you—are you the pigeon lady?"

Callie pointed dramatically at him. "I am the pigeon lady."

He whooped. "Brilliant. My nan voted for UKIP last time the Mayoral elections happened, but she's obsessed with your TikToks. Keep going!"

As the jogger disappeared into the mist of tourist buses and Brexit-weary traffic, Jordan whispered, "I think we've crossed into cult status. We should start issuing robes."

"Only if they're neon and sequinned," Callie said, watching as the last few pigeon confetti shapes drifted lazily into the Thames, catching the sunlight like stained glass in motion. "Let's pack down before someone sends the riot ducks."

* _ * _ * _ *

"Yo, its Monday, and here's another Callie Hall show, here on Manic Radio Essex," Callie said into the microphone. She knew that it was necessary to pre-record her show, instead of being live, as Robert had told her that both OFCOM and the Electoral Commission were now watching every live second of her output with the intensity of a ravenous hawk watching a chipmunk riding a unicycle. The message was clear: no unvetted chaos on live radio. But nobody said she couldn't pre-record the chaos and pretend it was live.

"Coming up," she continued smoothly, seated in Studio 4 at the Olympic Park hub, "we've got the latest in legal gossip, party poppers outside Parliament, and maybe—just maybe—a promise to outlaw lanyards if I win this bloody thing. But first, here's the news across Essex."

Callie knew that doing voice tracking, a common technique among commercial DJs to give the illusion of being live, was both her safety net and her subversive playground. She could pre-record just enough edge to keep OFCOM calm while still sounding like she was causing controlled anarchy in real time.

The red light above the studio door flicked off, indicating her mic feed was off. Callie leaned back in her chair, spinning it with a low groan as she stretched.

Daisy poked her head in. "How was that for a revolution in under two minutes?"

Callie thumbed her headphones off. "Tidy. Got the dig in at Jenkins, squeezed in the promise about lanyards, and even managed a callback to the Parliament pigeons."

Daisy crossed the room and flopped into the other chair, still wearing the same feather earrings from that morning's Bridge Blitz. "You realise Lord Gold has become a full-on cult figure in the Discord server, right? Someone's already photoshopped him riding a giant pigeon over the Houses of Parliament with the caption 'Lord of the Wings.'"

Callie cackled. "He'll bloody love that."

A beat passed between them. The buzz of the studio quieted just enough for Daisy to say, "Have you seen this?"

She pulled out her phone and slid it across the desk. It was open to a headline from The Telegraph:

HALL'S HIGH-FLYING CAMPAIGN BREACHES 'RESPECTABILITY BARRIER' — TORIES LOSING GROUND AMONG YOUTH VOTERS IN GREATER LONDON.

Callie read it twice, her smirk slowly creeping back. "We've breached the respectability barrier? Mate, that sounds like something I want on a bloody plaque."

"Yeah, well, according to The Telegraph, you've also breached the patience of several borough councillors, one bishop, and the management team at Capital FM."

"They should try therapy," Callie said, leaning forward again and tapping at her show rundown on the screen. "Better yet, they should try a night out at Sticky's 'Graff and Bass' night in Peckham. Full emotional reset guaranteed."

"Speaking of emotional resets," Daisy said, pulling out another flyer, this one a printed email. "Got a reply from the Electoral Commission about your appeal to let DJ Pigeon be your official campaign mascot on the ballot paper."

Callie took it, scanning the overly formal language before collapsing into laughter. "'We regret to inform you that animal or anthropomorphised cartoon mascots cannot represent candidates on the London Mayoral ballot.' Bloody killjoys."

"But they did say," Daisy said, pulling out a second sheet, "that if DJ Pigeon formally changes their name by deed poll to a human identity, they could technically stand for Assembly."

Callie raised her eyebrows. "Are you telling me Tash could legally run for the London Assembly as..."

She paused, her voice full of gleeful menace.

"...Diane J. Pigeon?"

Daisy nodded. "And you're telling me you don't want to see her in a debate with Sadiq Khan?"

"I want nothing more in my life," Callie said solemnly. "Make it happen."

* _ * _ * _ *

James Jenkins was in hell. And his hell was beige.

The colour of the boardroom walls. The stale shortbread biscuits laid out on a tray like a sad buffet. The Excel spreadsheet glowing on the central projector. Beige, beige, beige. And none of it doing a single thing to cool the rage simmering in his temples.

Across the table, three executives from Global's PR arm were mid-way through explaining how not reacting to Callie Hall's latest stunt was actually a form of strategic dominance.

"So," one said, pinching the bridge of his nose, "we let her have her moment. It's a meme, it's ephemeral. By Wednesday, the news cycle's moved on. She's just pigeons and glitter, not a real threat."

"She's polling ahead of our preferred Conservative candidate in Walthamstow," James snapped, pointing at the latest YouGov figures. "And she's three points behind Labour in Barking. Barking!"

A junior analyst who'd been desperately pretending not to exist looked up. "She is very popular on TikTok."

James's eyes narrowed. "Do you know how much of Global's advertising base relies on not appealing to TikTok users? Do you know what happens when our brand is mocked by literal schoolchildren armed with Adobe Premiere and a vendetta against Heart FM's Top 40?"

The room was silent.

James stood abruptly, pacing toward the window that overlooked Leicester Square. The statue of Shakespeare stared back at him, indifferent and immortal, as if to say, even I couldn't write this shit.

"I want her neutralised," he said at last. "I want the Battle Bus off the streets. I want her campaign classed as a public nuisance. I want her YouTube channel demonetised, her TikTok flagged, and her radio show banned. After all, if Farage had to stand down while running a broadcast operation, so should she, especially as the Manic Collective is classed as a political party as its registered under the Electoral Commission."

One of the PR executives coughed into his hand. "Actually… about that…"

James turned, his glare sharp enough to cut through reinforced contracts.

The PR man continued, visibly sweating. "We… looked into that precedent. Ofcom ruled that as long as she's not using *regulated* broadcast airtime to solicit votes, and as long as the content is editorially separate from the campaign arm of the party, it's… allowed."

"Allowed?" James thundered. "She's using the airwaves to call me the Emperor of Beige and claiming our radio empire is run by zombies who cry when you play Bicep!"

"Well... legally speaking, she's not saying that as a candidate. She's saying it as a 'drive-time personality with a highly exaggerated media persona'... it's editorially distinct."

James stared at them all, his fists clenched at his sides. "You mean to tell me I've spent twenty-two years weaponising compliance manuals, and now the biggest threat to our dominance is someone in a pigeon onesie dancing on a bridge to a Spotify playlist?"

A different analyst—a brave one, perhaps too brave— offered gently, "She also has 4.3 million views on her clip of launching biodegradable pigeons. That's more reach than all of our London stations combined last week..."

Silence.

James picked up the biscuit tray and hurled it across the room. It hit the whiteboard with a soft, pitiful clatter. Crumbs rained onto the floor.

"Get out," he said through gritted teeth. "Get. Out. Of. My. Sight."

The room emptied with the efficiency of a fire drill.

Alone, James dropped into his chair, staring at the enormous stack of legal folders on his desk. He pressed the intercom.

"Timothy?"

A frightened voice crackled back. "Yes, sir?"

"I want an emergency legal conference call with the Electoral Commission, Ofcom, and the BBC standards board. If she breathes out of sync with a campaign jingle, I want her shut down."

"Of course, sir."

"Oh, and Timothy?"

"Yes?"

"My wife and I are on holiday from tomorrow for the rest of the week, and I've forgot to book a flight. Get me a PanEuro flight to Nice Côte d'Azur and a helicopter shuttle to Monaco. Executive Class from Manston. Use my credit card."

"Already done, sir," Timothy replied, barely masking the tremor in his voice. "I booked the 08:10 AM departure. You'll have Champagne on take-off and clearance through Fast Track."

James grunted his approval.

"And the hotel?"

"The Fairmont, sir. Presidential suite. Secluded. Sea view. All expenses charged to your account."

James allowed himself a flicker of relief. Monaco. Quiet. Order. No pigeons. No DJs. No glitter. Just him, Carly, and the luxurious cocoon of people who only pretended to care.

Yet even as he visualised the white tablecloths and sea breezes, something inside gnawed at him. He had spent two decades pulling the levers of British media and law, reshaping the public square into something controllable. Polished. Predictable. Beige. And now, somehow, it was all being unravelled by someone who used "vibes" as a manifesto plank.

****

CHAPTER 16 - Debating Things the Day Before

Wednesday 1st May 2024

The Barbican-style bowl that Manic Radio owned, underneath the Olympic Park studios and normally used by Manic Classical and Manic Jazz—the two 'highbrow' stations within the ever-chaotic Lite Group empire—was hastily transformed into a debate venue. Velvet-covered stools replaced traditional orchestral seating, while AV interns, normally in charge of mixing Mahler and modal jazz, frantically calibrated sound desks for political microphones.

There was something undeniably surreal about it. The sweeping concrete walls, built to reflect cello resonance, now echoed with the nervous coughs of mayoral candidates and the low hum of badly hidden TikTok livestreams. The irony that the debate amongst all of the Mayoral candidates, held on the evening prior to the biggest vote in the capital's calendar, was taking place in a place where culture, class and cohabited peacefully was not lost on the Manic Radio interns. One of them, wearing a hoodie with "MOZART BUT MAKE IT MANIC" scrawled across the back in Sharpie, tiptoed around wires like they were tripwires in a Bond film.

The irony, Callie knew, that it was scheduled for half past 7, only half an hour after she had been scheduled, on a normal day, to be finishing her drive time show. Of course, as she was a candidate, and Romford, a London Borough, was within the Manic Radio Essex broadcast patch, she had been taken off air for the week "to maintain neutrality." She'd responded by publishing a now-viral TikTok in which she declared neutrality to be "a bourgeois construct upheld by the BBC and their collection of sad ties," before cutting to a clip of her own slogan looped over a sped-up remix of the "Thomas the Tank Engine" theme.

Still, she had dressed in a modicum of restraint for the occasion. The usual leather jacket and slogan tee had been replaced by a cropped red blazer, strategically unbuttoned just enough to reveal a laminated "VOTE MANIC" lanyard and the top of a sequinned camisole that glinted under the floodlights. Her DJ headphones, still slung around her neck, were perhaps a step too far, but she refused to relinquish them. "Part of the brand," she'd muttered, when Daisy begged her to leave them in the green room.

Looking around as she took part in the sound checks, she counted, alongside herself, 14 candidates, from Sadiq Khan for Labour, Susan Hall for the Conservative party, Howard Cox for Reform UK and even London Real's Britain First joining the debate, led by Manic Radio's CEO, Adam Banks, the former promotions manager for Brookes Vibes back in the early 2000s, who was wearing a suit and dodgy pair of Converse, and had somehow managed to sneak a Red Bull into his inside pocket despite the "no energy drinks on stage" rule imposed by the in-house events coordinator.

The event had been advertised as being open to the London public, as it was seen as a 'public engagement' session, a dodge by Manic used for its requirements that OFCOM had laid out in the various licence and broadcasting guidelines it had cleverly interpreted with the help of a freelance barrister who moonlit as a spoken word poet in Camden. In reality, however, it was more politics students, die hard Labour and Tory voters, and City Hall employees from the team who dealt with elections and democracy services, who were there to ensure compliance with electoral law and to furiously scribble notes whenever someone went a syllable over their allotted time. The rest of the seats were filled by a smattering of invited guests, suspiciously media-friendly influencers, and Steve Bray, who was known for standing outside Parliament with a megaphone and shouting about Brexit. Callie had no doubt that, somehow, Steve would find his way into the spotlight by the end of the evening.

Waiting for her cue to enter the stage, Callie knew that it would be a bit different to normal debates, as the entrances of each candidate was to be like wrestling entrances, where each candidate would enter the stage to a track that their campaign team had selected. Callie knew what hers was, as, with the pigeon being her emblem, she had picked the theme from Dastardly and Muttley's "Catch the Pigeon," an old Hanna-Barbera cartoon theme that was equal parts nostalgic and ridiculous. The reason she had picked that was simple, it was because the whole "Klunk, you invent me a thingamabob that catches that pigeon or I'll lose my job" line was one of the few things that had ever made her laugh at her own absurdity. The cartoon's absurd attempts to catch an invincible pigeon reflected her own chaotic campaign and her penchant for challenging the status quo.

If I'm going to disrupt, she thought, *why not make it utterly ridiculous while still making a point?*

As the evening unfolded, Callie's nerves were oddly absent, replaced by the electric anticipation of what was about to transpire. The velvet-covered stools and concert hall acoustics were an intentional clash with the reality of a high-octane, lowbrow campaign. The debate was being broadcast to an eager and often incredulous public, ready to absorb whatever chaos came their way.

Daisy, standing in the wings, flashed Callie a thumbs-up as the candidate queued up for her entrance. Callie turned to face the stage with a confident grin, adjusting her red blazer as her fingers reflexively grazed the edges of the laminated "VOTE MANIC" lanyard hanging at her neck. The sequence was set, and as expected, the theme from Dastardly and Muttley began to blare out across the room.

The screech of the brass section opening with a raucous flair coincided with Callie's dramatic entrance. She strode onto the stage with a playful yet determined swagger, head held high, her headphones hanging defiantly from her neck. A smile played at the corner of her lips as the crowd's mixed reactions washed over her. Some snickered at her theatrics, others applauded, and a few wore expressions of utter disbelief, no doubt wondering what exactly they had signed up for.

In the front row, Steve Bray—ever the disruptor himself—was already waving a placard that read, "Who Needs a Mayor When You Have Pigeons?" Callie raised an eyebrow at the sight of him, half-amused, half-resigned. She would have to contend with the political oddities of London's protest scene tonight, but that was nothing new.

As the other candidates made their entrances, each one more subdued than Callie's, she found herself scanning the room, trying to size up her competitors. Sadiq Khan was entering with his usual charisma, his supporters applauding loudly as his campaign anthem—some earnest, synth-heavy track—played in the background. Howard Cox for Reform UK, with his trademark passion for deregulation, was next, his entry marked by a quirky song selection that only someone with a peculiar sense of humour would dare choose: "I Want to Break Free" by Queen. The whole thing had an air of out-of-touch absurdity that made it hard not to laugh.

Callie's gaze then moved to Britain First's representative, a figure who seemed to blend in with the background despite the controversy of their party. Their entrance track was a jarring contrast to the others—"Rule Britannia!"— and it was clear that their campaign was banking on nostalgia and divisiveness rather than forward-thinking policies.

In the moments before the debate truly began, Adam Banks took the stage, his Converse trainers tapping a rhythm on the concrete stage, signalling the start of the event. The lights dimmed slightly as he welcomed the candidates with an exaggerated flourish, drawing chuckles from the audience. His words were intentionally dramatic, almost absurd, as if to match the chaos of the evening.

"Ladies and gentlemen, and those who are merely here for the spectacle, welcome to the Great Mayoral Debate of 2024! If you're listening on East London Hits, London Vibes, South London Vibes or North London Vibes, then

I'm sorry that you won't be hearing Toni Green on Manic Prime Evenings, our evening show, and instead are listening to something that will likely be even more chaotic than our usual fare."

Adam then paused, and Callie noticed he was looking at his script, obviously as he'd never done something like this, as he was more of a desk based and promotions guy, not a presenter, not a broadcaster, unlike her.

"Tonight, we have the political spectacle of a lifetime, featuring 14 candidates, each vying for your votes. Forget about boring policy talks and dry speeches—tonight is about true political engagement. We'll be putting each of you through the wringer, asking questions that matter, but also letting you answer with whatever ridiculousness comes to mind. After all, if we wanted a traditional debate, we would have just aired a rerun of The Thick of It. But no, we're here for something new, something real, and something very Manic."

The audience laughed, and Callie felt her nerves settle. This wasn't going to be like any debate she'd ever seen before. It was going to be messy, unpredictable, and most importantly, entertaining. If they weren't here for policy, they were certainly here for the theatre, and she was prepared to give them exactly that. As Banks made his final remarks, he introduced the format: each candidate would have a chance to make an opening statement, after which they would be subjected to a series of rapid-fire questions. The audience would vote on who performed best in each segment, and those results would be announced in real-time.

"Without further ado," Banks continued, "Let's begin with the opening statements. First up, it's the incumbent, the Labour Party's Sadiq Khan."

Callie had to chuckle at how all 14 candidates were seated on the stage, chairs that were usually used for Manic's in-vision podcasts with microphones by each chair and a small table next to each with space for a glass of water, notes and a phone that no one would be looking at, not unless they were completely unprepared or playing some twisted game of "political poker." The setup was a clear indication that this was going to be unlike any formal debate. There was no podium for grand speeches or heavy-handed lecturing, just candidates on velvet stools under stark lights, playing by the rules of Manic Radio—chaos with a purpose.

Callie knew the running order for the opening statements, as it was being done based on party share of votes at the previous election. This meant that Sadiq Khan, as the incumbent, would go first, and she, as a representative of a brand new party, like the Reform and Real London candidates, would be the final ones to speak, as the independents, people who had no party backing, had theoretically came 5th in the 2021 election and were thus placed following the Greens and Liberal Democrats in 5th to speak. Callie had specifically asked to go as the very final candidate, knowing the importance of leaving a lasting impression on both the audience and the viewers listening on their radios, or watching the Kick stream that Manic had set up.

"Why Kick and not Twitch or YouTube?" Callie had asked, curious, before the event. Daisy had shrugged and replied, "Because, apparently, it's more 'Manic'—whatever that means."

Callie's lips quirked in amusement as the first candidate, Sadiq Khan, launched into his opening statement, his voice smooth and confident. He ticked all the usual boxes—his record as Mayor, his promises for affordable housing, and his commitment to tackling the climate crisis. His performance, polished and professional, would undoubtedly win the votes of many in the room. But Callie knew that wasn't her game.

She wasn't here to simply "tick the boxes." She was here to tear down the idea of what a mayor should be, to challenge every established expectation and ridicule the very concept of the political elite. And she would do that with all the flair, absurdity, and spectacle she could muster.

As each candidate made their opening statements, Callie leaned back slightly in her velvet stool, watching the dynamics unfold. Susan Hall from the Conservative Party followed Khan, presenting a far more conservative, no-nonsense approach, focusing on law and order and the importance of traditional values. Howard Cox for Reform UK was up next, a maverick in his own right, advocating for deregulation and less government interference, his passion for free-market capitalism shining through every word. Then came the oddity of Britain First, whose representative delivered an uncomfortable diatribe that seemed straight out of a 1950s colonial Britain fantasy. The audience winced, and Callie fought to suppress her own reflexive scoff.

Each candidate's performance seemed more ordinary than the last, and she couldn't help but wonder if they truly understood the circus they were part of. This wasn't a platform for dry speeches and promises to build more homes or lower taxes—it was a stage for something raw, something chaotic. And she was going to make sure that she brought exactly that.

Finally, it was her turn. Adam Banks had called her name with the same dramatic flair he had used for every other candidate, his voice booming across the room.

"Last but certainly not least, the candidate who may or may not have been 'cancelled'—the one, the only, Callie Hall!"

The crowd's mixed reaction rang in her ears as she stood up from her stool, straightened her red blazer, and strode confidently to the centre of the stage. The theme from Dastardly and Muttley blared through the speakers again, and she couldn't help but smile at the absurdity of it all.

She took her seat, adjusted her headphones, and then, without missing a beat, leaned into the microphone and spoke.

"Good evening, London. My name is Callie Hall, and I am here to tell you that I'm not like the other candidates on this stage, and I'm damn proud of it," she began, her voice clear and unapologetic. "I'm not here to pretend that I know exactly how to fix the housing crisis, or that I've got all the answers to climate change. What I do know is that London needs a shake-up. A revolution, if you will. And what better way to do that than with a DJ pigeon mascot, an old bus covered in graffiti, and a campaign slogan that makes absolutely no sense? The truth is, all the promises you've heard tonight—whether it's more housing, fewer regulations, or making London 'great again'—they're just words. Words from politicians who think they've got it all figured out. But they don't. No one has it figured out. Not Sadiq, not Susan, not Howard, not anyone on this stage. So why not vote for something different? Something that doesn't make sense? Someone who wants to ban Capital and give free WKD to all Uni students? Someone who wants, and this will make Tim Martin ill, to nationalise Wetherspoons!"

A sudden chant from the Politics students of "FREE WKD!" made Callie grin, her words bouncing off the velvet walls. It wasn't polished, it wasn't conventional, but it was real, and the room knew it. This was the magic of her campaign. No one else could bring the same blend of irreverence, humour, and complete disdain for the rules of traditional politics.

As the chant died down, Callie pressed on, undeterred.

"Because let's be honest here: I'm from Romford, Zone 6, meaning unlike my learned friend... yeah, I'm using politics terms, clever me! I've actually lived in a place where people don't give a toss about the latest policy trends or which policy paper Sadiq Khan has got from a bunch of think tanks. You can tell me all about housing crisis numbers or climate pledges, but I know that people need real change, not more of the same political drivel. And that change doesn't come in the form of another guy in a suit telling you that everything's going to be fine, it comes in the form of a pigeon who listens to music and spins the decks!"

The audience reacted, some laughing, others unsure whether to take her seriously. That was the trick. Callie wasn't there to be taken seriously; she was there to get people thinking, to disrupt the status quo and, more importantly, to make them question why they were following the same old script. Her speech wasn't about answers—it was about sparking something far more powerful: doubt.

Callie paused for a moment, letting the room settle as her words began to hang in the air. It was almost as though the sheer chaos of her campaign was bleeding into the space itself—every corner filled with tension, anticipation, and a slight touch of disbelief. She could feel the eyes of the audience on her, some curious, some perplexed, but all waiting for the next line to make sense of what she had just said.

"Look," she continued, leaning slightly forward, her voice dropping a notch to emphasise the sincerity, "if you want the same old political speeches, you've got plenty of choices. If you want someone who tells you they've got it all figured out, then yeah, go ahead and vote for a politician who's just recycling the same old nonsense. But if you're tired of hearing empty promises and watching the same thing play out over and over again, well, I've got an offer for you: Vote for the pigeon. Vote for chaos. Vote for unpredictability, because that's what this city needs."

The crowd was a strange mix of laughter and applause, but Callie knew she had landed the point. The words had stuck, and now she just needed to keep riding that wave of energy. She wasn't sure if anyone truly believed she was a viable candidate, but that was irrelevant at this stage. She was here to shake the very foundations of how politics was played. To challenge the idea that a mayor should be some polished, untouchable figure. To show that the public didn't need another suit-and-tie individual promising grand reforms that would take decades to implement. No, they needed something different. Something bold, something ridiculous, and something with enough swagger to break the monotony.

"Thank you Callie, now, we'll get down to the nitty gritty, but first, we want to know, from each candidate," Adam said, grinning, "if you were an animal, which would you be and why?"

* _ * _ * _ *

By time 10pm came, Callie was worn out, as, even though there had been breaks at 8pm and every half hour, short, 5 minute breaks, which she knew were for the news and ads to be aired on London Vibes and its sister stations, her mind was buzzing. She was a mixture of exhausted and exhilarated, feeling both drained from the onslaught of questions and invigorated by the spectacle of the night. The debate had gone longer than expected, with the final round of rapid-fire questions, each one designed to catch the candidates off guard, pushing everyone to their limits, and the closing statements, which had just concluded, allowing the candidates a final chance to make their mark. The audience had been unpredictable, a mixture of those genuinely interested in the issues, and those simply waiting to see how the chaos would unfold.

"Well folks, that's the end of that," Adam said at 9:59pm, and Callie knew that he was about to lead into the 10pm news and the late evening network show that Manic aired after Manic Prime Evenings with Toni Green. The energy in the room was palpable, but now it was over. Callie felt a mix of triumph and exhaustion. The night had been an absolute whirlwind, a chaotic blend of soundbites, absurdity, and moments of unexpected clarity. She had given her all in the debate, not just in the speeches but in the way she carried herself—an unapologetic force in the middle of a political circus. "I'd like to thank everyone listening on Manic Radio, no matter if you're listening on FM, DAB, the Manic Prime app, or on smart speaker, everyone watching on Kick, or in the audience here today. Remember that tomorrow, if you're going out to vote, you'll need ID as well as your ballot card to make it easier for polling station staff, and on Saturday, we'll be live from City Hall when the announcement is set to be made about who will be the next Mayor of London. But for now, let's enjoy the rest of the evening. Thanks for staying with us."

The lights dimmed, and the candidates began to filter off the stage, some chatting amongst themselves, while others were deep in thought. Callie stood at the edge of the stage for a moment, allowing the final moments of the chaotic debate to settle in her mind. The energy from the crowd, the flurry of questions, the strange mixture of mockery and intrigue—it had all coalesced into something surreal, something that couldn't be easily explained. But that was the point. She wasn't here to be understood in the conventional sense. She was here to break apart the carefully constructed veneer of politics and offer something raw, something real, something that could be remembered.

As she made her way to the green room, Daisy approached her with a wide grin.

"You did it," Daisy said, her eyes sparkling. "That was brilliant. The crowd loved it. You made them think, Callie. You didn't just give them policy; you gave them something they can't ignore."

Callie smiled, still catching her breath. "Yeah, I think I did. I didn't even have to try to be outrageous. It's just… who I am."

"I know," Daisy said, her voice playful. "But, seriously, that pigeon thing? Genius. It'll stick with them. People are going to remember that."

Callie leaned back against the wall and closed her eyes for a brief moment. "It's weird, isn't it? The idea of being remembered for a stupid mascot and a broken bus. But I think that's the point. People want something different. They don't want the same old speeches and promises. They want change, but they want it in a way they can feel, not just hear."

Daisy chuckled, adjusting her jacket as she paced around the room. "And I think that's exactly what you're giving them. Whether they vote for you or not, Callie, you've sparked something. That was chaos with a purpose."

****

CHAPTER 17 – The Shuttle Buses
Thursday 2nd May 2024

Callie was sat on the Manic Battle Bus, but this time she wasn't actively campaigning—because it was election day. Instead of using the Battle Bus to campaign for votes, she had rebranded it for the day as a voter transport shuttle.

Using that, and 33 sixteen- to thirty-seater buses hired for the day from an Essex-based company that normally did private hires for hen dos, school trips and the occasional Chelmsford dog show, she had funnelled the remaining £25,000 of the campaign budget into a hastily organised, slightly chaotic, but ultimately functional "Get Out The Vote" operation.

Not all 33 were being used in East London.

No, there was one in each of the boroughs, plus a handful doing loops through marginal estates and commuter zones in Havering, Barking, and Bexley. Callie had even managed to wrangle two buses to cover isolated outposts of outer London where public transport was notoriously unreliable—places like Harold Hill, Thamesmead West, and parts of Dagenham that the night bus forgot.

"You know, Callie, technically you're only supposed to offer transportation to the polling stations, not bribe the voters with free WKD Blue and ironic bingo cards," Manic's legal advisor, Robert Hollis, muttered down the line, sounding like he was wedged somewhere between a migraine and a coronary.

Callie, sat cross-legged in the jump seat of the Manic Battle Bus, now converted into a rolling voter shuttle, swirled her half-empty energy drink and gestured vaguely out the window.

"They're not bribes, Robert," she said brightly, eyes fixed on the queue forming outside the polling station at the Romford Greyhound Track. "They're… morale boosters. Spirits of democracy. Liquid enthusiasm, if you will."

"The Electoral Commission won't see it that way," Robert sighed. "You've already pushed the boundaries with the Battle Bus being parked near polling stations, and now I'm hearing your lot handed out bingo cards where one of the squares said 'Vote while drunk on WKD.'"

Callie snorted. "It says 'Vote while tipsy'. Very different vibe."

Robert groaned. "Callie, please, for the love of electoral legality, don't end up being struck off the ballot after people have voted for you."

"Relax, Robbie," she said, sipping from a paper cup of warm, deeply questionable coffee. "We're running a parallel transport network because TfL's running at half-speed in Zone 6 and no one under thirty-five knows where their polling station is. You should be giving me a bloody knighthood."

"Ah, so you're using the 'providing transport to voters so they can do their civic duty' get out of jail free card," Robert said, his voice tight with resignation. "I suppose I should be grateful you didn't rig up DJ Pigeon on the roof to fire confetti every time someone flashed their polling card."

There was a pause. Callie looked down at her phone guiltily, her thumb hovering over a paused TikTok draft.

"…you didn't," Robert said, flatly.

"Erm… I was tempted to. I did ask all the bus drivers to play Capital though… as loud as they could… to annoy the passengers," Callie then said, grinning. "You see, if they're annoyed with Capital, they'll vote for anything just to feel better about their day. It's called 'strategic discomfort'," she added, her tone as serious as she could muster, but the grin never left her face.

"I can't believe this is happening," Robert muttered under his breath, before a loud sigh followed. "Look, just make sure you don't cross any more lines today. We've been over this."

"Sure thing, Robbie," Callie said, tapping her phone screen absently as she stared out the window at the mix of supporters and disinterested passersby milling about the polling station. "Don't worry, no more confetti cannons... today."

With a final exhausted sigh, Robert hung up, leaving Callie to her thoughts. The Battle Bus, which had once been a symbol of chaotic energy and youthful rebellion, now had a new purpose: the city's unofficial, yet extremely practical, election-day shuttle. It was an odd sight—"Vote for Callie Hall" slogans plastered across the side of the bus, but with a gleaming row of seats filled with silent commuters rather than enthusiastic supporters.

"Right," she said to Hammond, who was in the driver's seat, grinning. "We're going to the London School of Economics next, give the horn a good blast when we pull in. Remind them it's democracy day."

Hammond, clutching the battered wheel of the Manic Battle Bus, glanced up in the rear-view mirror and chuckled, clearly enjoying his newfound role as the day's unofficial democracy chauffeur.

"Will do, boss," Hammond replied, checking his mirrors and expertly guiding the Battle Bus out of the Romford Greyhound Track's overcrowded car park. "But no confetti?"

Callie shook her head with mock regret. "Nope. Robert Hollis said we're banned from confetti, balloons, or anything fun. Apparently, fun violates electoral regulations."

"Typical," Hammond laughed, swerving gently to avoid a group of voters who were shuffling reluctantly towards the polling station, faces buried in their phones.

As the Battle Bus rattled onto the A118 towards Stratford, Callie took a deep breath, feeling the strange weight of election day settle upon her shoulders. She wasn't used to this quieter side of campaigning, the sudden cessation of manic speeches and outlandish stunts. Instead, here she was, sitting cross-legged in a converted DJ booth, surrounded by a handful of quiet, thoughtful voters making their way to vote.

From the back of the bus, Daisy looked up from her laptop, smiling warmly. "You alright, Callie?"

"Yeah, just feels odd," Callie said softly, her gaze drifting out of the scratched windows as they passed through a tapestry of urban East London. "All these weeks of madness, and now we just wait."

"It's the quiet before the storm," Daisy said, tapping at the keys. "Socials are going nuts. The hashtag #VoteManic is still trending, and everyone's posting selfies from the shuttle buses."

Callie felt a flutter of warmth. "Really?"

"Yeah," Daisy grinned. "Turns out, people quite like democracy when it comes with a side of chaos."

Callie laughed, nodding as Hammond tooted the horn loudly at a group of builders drinking tea at a roadside café. They waved their polystyrene cups back cheerfully, a few giving exaggerated thumbs-ups.

By the time they pulled up outside the London School of Economics, a crowd of excitable students had already gathered, attracted by both the bus's garish colour scheme and the promise of transport to the polling stations. Hammond gave the horn several triumphant blasts, earning enthusiastic cheers and ironic applause from the students clustered around the kerb.

"Next stop—your polling stations! Let one of the Manic Mates know which is your allocated polling station, and we'll work out a route that takes you all exactly where you need to go!" Callie shouted over the excitable chatter of the crowd.

A girl with green hair and a battered vintage denim jacket elbowed her way to the front of the queue, raising a hand like she was in a seminar. "Are you Callie? Actual Callie Hall?"

"Last I checked," Callie replied, flashing a playful grin.

"Oh my God, iconic!" The girl quickly posed for a selfie, leaning close enough that her collection of enamel badges rattled softly against Callie's blazer. "My mum is literally voting for you just because you wound up Nick Ferrari live on air."

"I do my best," Callie laughed. "Jump aboard. We've got democracy to deliver."

As the throng of students crammed into the Battle Bus, Callie paused for a moment, breathing deeply. It was easy to joke around, easier still to poke fun at the pompous absurdity of modern politics—but in the brief quiet of election day, with the ballots now irrevocably marked by thousands of Londoners, the weight of it all was tangible. She'd made politics messy, silly, irreverent—she'd challenged convention at every turn. But now, all she could do was ferry voters from A to B and hope the disruption had stuck in the minds of enough people to make a difference.

Daisy hopped down beside her, phone still buzzing in her hand. "The buses are working perfectly. No major meltdowns yet, though Kez Mahoney just texted to say the bus in Southwark's been trashed by a load of locals with Chicken Cottage wrappers, and Toni Green's down here on the South Ruislip one and she said she swears she saw Boris Johnson boarding at the bus stop outside Wetherspoons.'"

Callie blinked. "The Boris Johnson?"

Daisy nodded, looking mildly alarmed but equally amused. "Yes, blonde mop and all. Apparently, he boarded, loudly declared he'd lost his Oyster card, then insisted on sitting up front and narrating the history of Uxbridge politics to the entire bus."

"Oh my god," Callie laughed incredulously. "Of course. Trust our buses to pick up stray former Prime Ministers. Hope he's having fun on the Manic Express."

Daisy rolled her eyes, smirking. "Kez is also begging for reinforcements down in Southwark. The Chicken Cottage situation sounds severe. He said the smell alone could drive voter turnout down single-handedly."

Callie shook her head, fighting the urge to giggle. "Democracy has never smelled so greasy. Anyway, I'm nipping upstairs, and whacking Capital on the audio setup, so we've got some counter-programming for the ride. Let's see how long it takes before someone demands we turn it off."

As Callie bounded up the stairs of the double-decker OB unit cum Battle Bus, she had to chuckle, as the set up was for a normal radio show that she could host, but also had 5G routers that allowed the RCS software used for broadcasting to uplink to the Lite Group cloud, making the Battle Bus a fully operational mobile studio. Hammond had even fixed the dodgy aux jack earlier that morning with electrical tape and a vague warning about "unpredictable feedback loops," but Callie was willing to risk it for the greater good—or at least a few minutes of irony.

She flicked a few switches, the screen glowing an angry red before calming to its default station carousel. There it was—Capital FM. She clicked it, waited for a second, and was rewarded with the blaring intro of yet another Calvin Harris remix, this one featuring someone called "Lil Peaché" and enough vocal processing to make an android blush.

Callie smirked. Perfect.

She leaned into the mic on the internal tannoy system and purred, "Ladies and gentlemen, welcome to the Capital Punishment segment of your voter shuttle journey. Remember, this is revenge for everyone who said, 'I don't do politics, I just vibe.' You want vibes? You've got vibes. Now sit back and suffer."

* _ * _ * _ *

"Right, Hammond, it's time we head to the Mecca Bingo in Eltham Hill," Callie said, looking at her phone and seeing it was half past one, meaning that the majority of pensioners would probably be finishing their games of bingo and might appreciate a lift to their polling stations. She stood, brushed her red blazer down, something that she didn't normally wear, as she usually wore a crop top and leggings, like most of Manic's female CHR hosts, and motioned for Hammond to start up the bus. He gave a casual thumbs-up from the driver's seat and revved the engine, the exhaust giving a throaty growl as the Battle Bus rumbled back onto the streets of East London.

As the bus began its journey towards Eltham Hill, Callie couldn't help but reflect on the events of the day. It had started out in a flurry of chaotic energy, but now, it felt quieter—less like a circus and more like a slow, deliberate game of chess. The voters were out there, walking to polling stations, checking in with their neighbourhood friends about their choices, or simply waiting for their turn at a ballot box.

But Callie knew better than most that politics was never just about the votes. It was about perception. She wasn't here to be a part of the establishment; she was here to shake it up. She'd pushed boundaries every step of the way. She'd made people laugh, made them think, and more than anything, she'd made them question why they'd always accepted the same old political system.

"All right, we're approaching Eltham Hill," Hammond called from the front. "You sure you're ready for this one? It's the bingo crowd—can't promise they're as excited about DJ Pigeon as the LSE lot."

Callie rolled her eyes dramatically. "If they're not, I'm playing the one where Calvin Harris is being mixed with silence. That'll really wake them up."

Hammond chuckled, and they cruised through the streets, which were now buzzing with the low hum of everyday life, punctuated by the occasional hoot of horns from taxis and buses in a hurry to nowhere in particular. When they pulled up outside Mecca Bingo, it looked like the ideal spot for one of Callie's signature photo ops—vibrant, chaotic, and slightly out of place. A few elderly patrons were trickling out, a collection of handbags, shopping bags, and bright knitted scarves in tow. Some were grumbling about the weather, others chatting about their wins or losses, all of them slightly distracted by the large, garish Battle Bus now idling at the curb.

"Ladies, have you voted yet?" Callie asked to the confused pensioners who were looking up from their bags and murmuring to each other.

A woman with bright red lipstick and an emerald-green scarf tilted her head curiously as she approached the bus. "What's all this, then? What's this bus doing here? Is it a disco?"

Callie grinned, stepping down from the bus with her best PR smile plastered on her face. "No disco today, love, but I can promise you something almost as good—free rides to your polling stations. It's Election Day, and we're here to make sure you get your vote for Mayor of London in."

The woman raised an eyebrow, clearly sceptical but intrigued. "A free ride? From a bus like this? What's the catch?"

"There's no catch, just a chance to make sure everyone gets their voice heard," Callie replied, pointing upwards at the large "Vote for Callie Hall" sign plastered across the roof of the Battle Bus. "You just need to make sure you have your ID on you, and you haven't already voted, and we'll take you to the polling station your polling card says you have to go. Even if it's the other side of London, we'll take you there. No hassle, no fuss, just democracy on wheels."

The woman squinted at Callie's face, clearly weighing the offer. Then, with a shrug, she said, "Well, I suppose that's nice of you. It's not every day you get offered a lift in a brightly coloured bus."

"Exactly!" Callie exclaimed, her grin widening. "It's all about making the process as fun as possible, and, trust me, a ride like this is an experience you'll be talking about for years."

By now, a small group of pensioners had gathered around the bus, all looking equally intrigued but uncertain. Callie could practically see the wheels turning in their heads as they contemplated the idea of hopping on this chaotic election-day shuttle.

"Come on, love, we've got more to get to," one woman, who seemed to be the most vocal of the group, said as she waved her hand dismissively at the others. "It's not like we've got anything better to do, and they're offering a free ride to the polling station."

"That's the spirit!" Callie cheered. "Let's make your vote count. You're a key part of the decision, you know."

The woman smiled, her face softening as she approached the bus, and soon the others followed. Callie had a few moments to chat with the group while they climbed aboard, offering to take a photo for one of the women who was proudly showing off her "I Voted" sticker.

As they all settled in, Hammond gave the bus a rev, clearly enjoying the unexpected thrill of playing both driver and unofficial ambassador of democracy. The group of pensioners, some of whom had never stepped foot on a bus like this before, began to loosen up, laughing about the absurdity of the situation. Callie could hear them gossiping about the other candidates as they made their way down the narrow aisle of the bus.

"Did you hear what Sadiq said about traffic congestion? The cheek of it!" one woman remarked to another.

"Ah, don't get me started on that woman from the Tories. She'd be lucky if she could even spell the word 'housing crisis,'" said another, shaking her head.

Callie smirked to herself. She wasn't just ferrying voters; she was offering a much-needed escape from the standard political rhetoric. The fact that she had become a part of their world, even if only for a fleeting moment, made all the ridiculousness of the day worthwhile.

* _ * _ * _ *

"You going to the Polling Station at Hackney Wick?" Callie heard from someone who was asking a Manic Mate, one of the street team, who had took over from Hammond at the wheel as they stopped outside Hackney Central Overground station. "I need to vote, and a mate said there were free buses to the polling stations. Is this it?"

It was half past 9, only half hour until the polling stations closed, and Callie had decided around 7pm to, instead of playing Capital on the streets, play Capital's sister station,

Capital Dance, the more energetic and clubby beats that seemed more fitting to the evening's vibe. The sound system hummed as she slid into the back of the bus again, glancing over at Daisy who had her phone glued to her ear, probably dealing with another social media crisis or questioning whether to post another ridiculous TikTok. But Callie knew better than to interrupt—today was all about keeping the wheels turning, literally and figuratively.

"Yeah, mate," 'Fat Tony', or Tony Harris as he was, said cheekily from the driver's cab. "We'll get you there and straight back in time to catch your bus home too!" He grinned at the passenger, a young man clutching a takeaway coffee cup, his eyes scanning the surrounding streets.

"Cheers, mate," the young man said, stepping aboard. He slumped into one of the seats with an exaggerated sigh, clearly grateful for the unexpected ride.

Callie smiled at the unfolding scene. It was chaotic, unpredictable, and absolutely *her* brand of madness. The buses had been running smoothly, though, much to her surprise. There had been minor hiccups—like the Southwark Chicken Cottage disaster—but nothing that had derailed the entire operation. She'd been fully expecting some sort of breakdown or scandal by now, yet the only thing out of place had been the absurdity of it all. She had managed to turn the logistical nightmare of running a transport network into a full-on electoral circus, complete with music, memes, and a highly questionable beverage offering.

"How's the turnout looking?" Callie asked Daisy, who had finally hung up from yet another call and was now typing furiously on her laptop.

Daisy glanced up briefly. "Solid, considering the last-minute push. Social media is alive with people heading to the stations in all areas. #VoteManic is trending still, and there's a steady stream of followers heading to polling booths after catching our buses." She paused, as if adding something more. "Kez is over in Bexley and says the energy is like a club, but with less neon and more old people complaining about how 'the Tories don't know what they're doing.'"

Callie snorted, leaning back against one of the bus's walls. "Sounds like democracy at its finest."

"That's one way of putting it," Daisy replied with a raised eyebrow. "There are definitely some interesting conversations happening on these buses. One lady just told Kez that she was 'voting for the pigeon' and she didn't even know what that meant, but it felt right."

"I'll take it," Callie said, her grin widening. "I don't care if they know what they're voting for. If they walk away feeling like they did something different, that's a win in my book."

They both fell into a brief silence, each processing the events of the day in their own way. It was nearing 10 p.m., and Callie could feel the weight of the hours spent running around, bouncing from polling station to polling station, ferrying voters, taking photos, all while trying to keep the absurdity of the whole operation from completely falling apart. Yet, despite the exhaustion, there was a strange exhilaration coursing through her. This chaotic campaign of hers might not win her the mayoralty, but it had certainly left an indelible mark.

Her eyes drifted toward the sound system, where the beats of Capital Dance now pounded through the bus. She felt a wave of satisfaction. It wasn't just about making noise—it was about making *them* listen. And whether or not they voted for her, Callie knew she'd made an impact. She'd made politics fun, she'd made it absurd, and most importantly, she'd made it *real* for people who had long ago tuned out of the usual drudgery.

"You sure you're ready for this?" Daisy asked, her voice breaking through Callie's musings.

Callie looked up at her, her mind suddenly clear. "Ready for what?"

Daisy gestured out the window at the growing crowd gathering outside the next polling station. The buses were now a vital part of the election-day landscape. They had become a mobile spectacle, just as much a symbol of the day as the ballots themselves. People were arriving at the polling station, some with uncertainty, others with excitement. A few even waved at the bus, cheering as it parked.

"To win or lose this thing, Callie," Daisy said, her voice low. "We're here now. Let's see where it goes."

Callie felt the weight of her words. It was surreal—her unconventional, chaotic campaign had brought her to this point, this exact moment. What did it mean to win, or to lose? In many ways, her entire run had been a protest against the very idea of winning politics. She wasn't a traditional candidate, and she didn't want to be. She wasn't here for promises or polished speeches. She was here for the people who felt forgotten by the mainstream, the ones who couldn't find themselves in the glossy, well-oiled machines of politics. The ones who liked a bit of disorder, a little mess, a lot of noise.

But there was still that little voice in the back of her mind, the one that wondered if it had been enough.

The young man who had gotten on at Hackney Central stood up, adjusting his oversized hoodie. "You're Callie, right?" he asked, his eyes wide with excitement. "I just wanted to say, I think you're doing an amazing job. Seriously, it's refreshing to see someone who actually gives a damn about the younger generation."

Callie blinked, slightly taken aback. "Wow, uh, thanks, mate. That means a lot."

He grinned, his energy infectious. "No worries. You're the only one who's actually *talking* to us. Like, you get it. You're shaking things up."

"Well," Callie said, rubbing her hands together, "that's what I'm here for."

****

CHAPTER 18 – Plans
Monday 6th May 2024

It had been two days since the results had been declared, two days since Sadiq Khan had been re-elected, for a third term, as Mayor of London, but Callie knew that her campaign had already made history—of the absurd, anarchic, and oddly influential kind. The headlines had barely begun to settle. MailOnline had run with "Callie's Carnival Ends in Confetti", while the Guardian had pondered, with a half-amused editorial, "Has the Gen Z Protest Vote Found Its Mascot?"

The Manic Battle Bus, now parked rather defiantly outside a Ladbrokes in Hackney Central, bore the scars of its long campaign: cracked fog lights, a dented nearside from an altercation with a Lime bike, and inexplicably, a traffic cone still wedged in its rooftop DJ booth. Daisy had tried to get it down with a broomstick. The cone had stayed, defiant as Callie's positioning in the results, 12th place, 1 vote ahead of Britain First, but behind Count Binface of all people. That fact alone had almost broken social media, that the Count Binface Party had gotten 24260 votes, she had got 20520 votes, Britain First had got 20519 votes, and podcaster Brian Rose of the Real London Party had gotten a mere 7501 votes, a total that triggered a rather embarrassing celebratory livestream on his part before someone informed him.

Callie hadn't stopped grinning since.

Not because she'd won, obviously, but because she had plans.

She had heard rumours that Nigel Farage was considering running for Parliament in a proposed General Election in Clacton, and Callie just happened to have an uncle who lived in the Essex seaside town, a fact which had not felt remotely relevant until now. With the Tories in absolute disarray, Labour clinging to their poll lead like a life raft in a Channel storm, and the Reform UK crowd starting to foam at the edges, Clacton was shaping up to be a flashpoint in the year to come. And Callie Hall had every intention of bringing a megaphone to it.

"You know, Daisy, I've had a mad idea..." Callie said with a grin that belonged more to a cartoon anarchist than a political candidate. She was sitting cross-legged on a leather seat of the Manic Battle Bus, nursing a can of Cherry Pepsi Max like it was a fine claret. "I'm going to see if the bosses will let me take this bus on tour to Clacton, and run... for MP in the next General Election."

Daisy, who was half-asleep with a Greggs sausage roll drooping from her mouth and one leg slung over the backrest of a broken seat, opened one bleary eye. "You want to… run for Parliament? In Clacton?"

Callie's grin widened. "Why not? I've got the momentum. I've got the bus. I've got the pigeon. And there's rumours a certain GB News host will be running as a Reform candidate."

Daisy stared at her friend like she'd just declared herself King of the Moon, chewing slowly. "Callie. Hun. You do realise that Clacton is basically Farage Disneyland, right? It's all Union Jack garden gnomes, retired colonels, and pensioners who think Jimmy Savile was framed."

Callie was unfazed. "Exactly! Perfect crowd for me. Think of it—a rave bus, a DJ pigeon, and the unapologetic chaos of the youth vote. It's like Glastonbury meets Question Time, and I'm headlining the mudslide stage."

"You placed twelfth," Daisy reminded her gently. "Behind a man with a bin on his head."

"Yes, but ahead of Britain First!" Callie shot back. "Which means there are at least twenty thousand Londoners who preferred vibes to fascism. That's a bloody mandate in my book. Anyway, you haven't heard my lead policies alongside banning Capital... I'm going to ban Gammon... and GB News."

Daisy blinked. "Ban... gammon?"

"Yep," Callie replied smugly, taking another sip of her Cherry Pepsi Max. "Gammon like Farage and his band of white-knuckled Kipper cultists, sitting there in their pub chairs, belching nationalism into their pint glasses while shouting at Carol Vorderman on Twitter. Gammon. Banned. Out. Done."

"You can't just ban gammon," Daisy mumbled, brushing pastry flakes from her hoodie. "It's a food. A processed pork product."

Callie leaned forward with the righteous energy of a uni politics fresher fuelled by Red Bull and delusion. "It's also a state of mind. A red-cheeked, Brexit-loving, faux-patriotic condition. I will introduce the Gammon Identification Act. If your blood pressure spikes when someone mentions Meghan Markle, you have to wear a high-vis sticker that says 'Do Not Engage—May Foam'."

Daisy snorted. "You'll have to create an entire department to manage that. A whole Ministry of Bants and Culture Wars."

*_*_*_*

It was time, Callie knew as she settled into Studio 25, one of the spare studios at the Olympic Park hub, as her usual studio, Studio 7, was offline due to technical reasons, with her drive show for Manic Radio Essex being moved to the spare space. She was prepped for another chaotic broadcast, but today, things were a little different. The studio, normally the domain of whimsical radio antics, was now an unexpectedly serene haven where Callie could fully contemplate her future—both political and broadcast. There was a subtle buzz in the air as news outlets had started calling her the "anti-politician of the year", and the attention had surged since the election results, despite the fact that she'd placed twelfth. Her laugh-out-loud antics, unfazed attitude, and undiluted energy had made her a memorable figure.

"How am I meant to take any of this seriously?" she muttered under her breath, as she adjusted the mic before going live.

Jordan was sitting on the other side of the desk, as opposed to the producers booth, where he had been spending most of his last few weeks trying to play the straight man to Callie's political antics. His brow furrowed as he adjusted his headphones, a slight tension in his posture as if the surreal and uncharted nature of Callie's campaign was beginning to settle in.

Callie, on the other hand, was wearing the grin of someone who had just realised that the entire system of politics was ripe for the taking—and she was the one to pluck the fruit.

Her mind was already racing ahead. The idea of Clacton was absurd, and that was exactly what made it brilliant. Clacton, a place famously identified with Farage, the Kippers, and all the archetypes of Brexit-fuelled fervour, would be the perfect stage for her next move. It was like a gift from the political gods—everything she hated, everything she could mock, and all the voters who, quite frankly, didn't know what they were missing.

With the 4pm news having finished and the opening promo sweeper having just aired, Callie tapped the mic with exaggerated reverence. "Alright, alright," she said with the sort of impish grin that could only be heard in her voice, "let's get this show rolling, yeah? Welcome back to the ride, folks, it's your girl Callie Hall on your 4-7 drivetime, here on Manic Essex. And if you're listening, we've got some real good gossip today. First up, though, we've got the all-new competition that everyone's been talking about, the £500k Money Drop. Yes, this Friday, Kyle and Sue on the early afternoon show are giving one lucky winner half a million quid."

"Yeah, and it's easy to enter," Jordan said, and Callie nodded, as she knew, along with Jordan, the script for the promos. "Well, Callie, all our listeners need to do is text DROP to 87106 or hop onto our website at manicradioplays.co.uk and click through to enter online. Entries cost £3, but there's also a free entry route, by calling 0330 880 3601, which is included in most phone plans. So, there's your chance, folks—£500,000 up for grabs, and with just a few taps or clicks, you could be in with a shot."

Callie flashed a grin, seamlessly adding, "Its a network competition across the Manic Prime network—so the competition is definitely heating up! Lines close this Friday at 3pm, and Kyle and Sue will phone one lucky winner live on-air to make their dreams come true. Anyway, we've got some Cardi B, some hotties from Southend who love Air Hostesses and Ed Sheeran coming up, along with some goss, but first, its Dua Lipa with Levitating, here on Manic Radio Essex, home to the diva, DJ Pigeon and someone who beat Britain First in the London Mayoral elections." Callie grinned, knowing she was about to dive into another round of absurdity that had made her a public favourite, and it seemed to be working. The chaotic energy that was Callie Hall was now as synonymous with Manic Essex as anything else, and with her new-found platform, there was no turning back.

The sound of Levitating playing out on the RCS Zetta system made Callie think about how she was going to have to get Robert to officially sign the papers for her Clacton campaign idea. It was a mad concept, but that was the point—disruptive, attention-grabbing, utterly ridiculous, and undeniably fresh.

As the track finished, Callie stood up, walking over to the control board, taking a deep breath before announcing her next move on air. "Alright, alright, alright, I'm feeling it today, people. How's everyone doing out there in Essex? Big shout-out to all my listeners in Southend, Chelmsford, and beyond. You're tuned into the chaos, and I'm Callie Hall, your Queen of Vibes."

She noticed Jordan's sceptical look. She could feel his hesitation, and a part of her understood why. After all, no one had ever quite seen anything like her campaign. It wasn't that Callie had planned for this madness; she hadn't—well, not at first. She'd launched into the mayoral race with the casual abandon of a woman who didn't fully grasp the seriousness of it. She'd used a ridiculous campaign bus, had a DJ pigeon as her mascot, and frankly, the whole thing was more about creating noise than any policy substance. Yet, in that noise, she had become something more than an internet meme.

"I've got a lot of things in the works," Callie continued into the mic, pacing across the room as she talked. "You know, after placing twelfth in the mayoral election, which, by the way, was one position ahead of Britain First—I've decided it's time for me to go bigger. No, seriously, folks. I'm going to stand for MP, but… I'm not going to reveal where just yet. Instead, I want you to WhatsApp me, 01245 960279 and tell me where you think in the Manic Radio Essex area I'm look at standing in, and I'll reveal all after half past 5. Let's just say, however, its somewhere that Capital will be persona non grata, and I'm bringing the noise, the vibes, and the only pigeon that matters with me. Up now, it's those hotties from Southend, James, Matt and Charlie, with an absolute banger, as here on Manic Radio Essex, it's What I Go to School For."

The sound of Busted's What I Go to School For blared through the speakers, its upbeat rhythm underscoring

Callie's electric energy as she paced the studio floor. The idea of announcing her next political move to the world was exhilarating, and she knew, deep down, this chaos was her best shot at securing a spot in the political limelight. It wasn't about playing by the rules—it was about bending, snapping, and downright obliterating the rules. And she was perfectly okay with that.

****

Books by Thomas Brant

Broadcasting Boundaries Series
BROADCASTING BOUNDARIES
BROADCASTING CHAOS
BROADCASTING DISRUPTION

The Wirral Gal Series
THE WIRRAL GAL... IN SPEKE
THE WIRRAL GAL... NOW A MAM

Other Stories in the Manic Radio Universe
THE BROOKES BABES
THE DAY THE QUEEN DIED
VIXEN
THE MANIC COLLECTIVE CANDIDATE

www.ingramcontent.com/pod-product-compliance
Lightning Source LLC
Chambersburg PA
CBHW031257120726
47906CB00003B/779